ACCIDENTAL P*RNSTAR

CINDY TANNER

Copyright © 2022 by Cindy Tanner

All rights reserved.

No part of this book may be reproduced in any form or by any electronic or mechanical means, including information storage and retrieval systems, without written permission from the author, except for the use of brief quotations in a book review. This is a work of fiction. Names, characters, places, and incidents are used fictitiously by the whims of the author imagination. Any resemblance to actual people, places, or things is purely coincidental.

To everyone brave enough to try waxing their delicate bits

1
TRIFECTA

The sweet, juicy apple turned sour on my tongue as I read the letter again. Forcing the bite past the sudden knot in my throat, I tried telling myself it wasn't that bad.

So, I'd just lost one of my two jobs. Mama Rosa had given me two hundred bucks cash and a family pan of lasagna with garlic bread as severance. I still had my part-time gig at the campus bookstore until the semester was over. I had some savings.

The budget cuts due to lack of funding causing me to lose the scholarship that covered the bulk of my tuition was a bigger problem. I could skip taking summer classes. It just meant not graduating early like I had worked hard for.

Taking a deep breath, I held it until my lungs started to burn.

This wasn't ideal, but it was manageable.

Fighting the urge to panic, I tossed the apple into the trash, telling myself the financial aid office wouldn't be open until Monday, so worrying would only ruin my weekend. A weekend that was now free since I no longer had shifts at the restaurant.

"You're home early." Chelsea's voice pulled my attention from the letter in my hand.

"Yup." I should probably mention it was because Mama Rosa was giving my job to her niece. She ran a small family-owned Italian bistro, so when her youngest niece had failed out of college and needed work, I was the only one on the payroll not in the family so I got the boot.

"Good. I need to talk to you, and we plan on going out later. Your part of the rent is going to be more, starting immediately."

"What?" I laughed, but the sound came out harsh.

"Ethan and I haven't been able to rent the extra room since Mason moved out. Now that we're engaged, we think it will be nice to have the space. It's going to be an extra three hundred a month. The check goes straight to me." Chelsea smiled and turned to leave, but my snort made her face me again.

"I live in a converted pantry that's under the stairs. I'm not paying you more money to live in a closet." I would be an idiot to when I could get an apartment for what she was now asking. Sure, utilities would be more, but I wouldn't be living like Harry Potter.

"You signed a lease. Did you forget my dad is a lawyer?" Chelsea cocked her hip out.

"I signed a lease to pay two hundred and fifty dollars a month, plus one quarter of the utilities until the end of the school year. Which happens to be this month." Standing, I ignore her.

"You always stay through the summer," Chelsea said so matter-of-factly that I winced because I wouldn't be this year. I would need to contact the registrar on Monday about dropping summer classes.

"Not for that price."

"Fine, you can move into the spare room upstairs, but it will be an extra hundred."

"I'm not paying you more money just because mommy and daddy won't pay for your wedding to a stoner with no future!" I snapped.

"I will sue you!" Chelsea screeched, repeating her favorite threat.

"How will you afford the legal fees?" I smirked, putting my hand up to stop her from stating the obvious. "Your dad specializes in elder law, not property, and I highly doubt he is going to take your side when he realizes you're trying to extort your last tenant." Snatching my book bag off the floor, I retreated to my tiny sanctuary, laughing as Chelsea stomped up the stairs.

Out of everything that had happened on this shitty ass day, this was the highlight. Which was sad considering it meant I had no other choice but move home for the summer. Maybe I could even commute from home and save on room and board next year.

It wasn't ideal, but it might work. If I didn't need any sleep. Laying back on my bed, staring at the weird slant of my ceiling, I hit Mom's number.

"Hey, mom." I forced my voice to sound chipper, even though I didn't feel it.

"How's my girl doing?" Mom sounded tired, her voice tugging at something in my chest.

"Good. I just got home from work. And it's Friday, so I survived another week!" I continued to force cheerfulness into my tone, glad I'd decided against a video call.

"Are you planning to come home soon?" Her tone hesitant, made me sit up.

"Finals are coming up." A new knot formed in my stomach. "Is everything okay?" Usually, I worked weekends, but that wasn't going to be an issue. My parents lived about two hours away, so it wasn't far, except when my almost twenty-year-old car was on empty and needed an oil change.

"You're still taking classes this summer, right?" Mom asked hesitantly, making me close my eyes. I really wasn't ready to admit defeat yet. "Your dad and I have something we want to tell you." In the background, I heard my dad's voice and mom mumbled out a not-so-empty threat about freezing his underwear if he spilled the beans before she did.

"Should I be worried?" I wondered what else today was going to dump on me. My parents were in their mid-forties and looked after their health, but suddenly, my mind spun a dozen different diagnoses.

"No, honey. I wanted to tell you in person, but I can't wait much longer. I've been hoping you'd surprise us with a visit." Dad's voice got louder in the background. Apparently, the threat of frozen tighty-whities wasn't a deterrent, but his words didn't sink in until mom repeated them.

"You're going to be a big sister!" Silence filled the other end of the line while I tried to process that, at twenty-one, I was getting a sibling.

"It wasn't planned." Mom laughed. "I hate to do this over the phone, but I know you stay busy. Your father and I are looking for a bigger place, but it might take some time, and I don't know if it will happen before the babies come."

Babies? Plural. Holy shit. I had to be developing some kind of stress-related auditory hallucinations.

"Twins, Juliet! We're having twins!" I heard dad yell in the background, making felt my mouth fall open. No, definitely not hallucinating.

"Don't you need to get to work?" Mom clucked her tongue in the way she did when she was aggravated as dad yelled a goodbye in the distance.

"Twins?" I was stunned.

"Your father and I always like doing things the hard way." Her laugh ended on a sigh, making my gut tighten. "I don't want you to feel like we're replacing you. Or that we're crazy people, but maybe use this as an example to use two forms of birth control. And even then, there are no guarantees. Unless it's anal."

"Mom. No." I laugh. "I don't have time to date anyway. I'll be fine."

"You don't have to date to get sex, Jules. A quick ten minutes is all it takes. I went to college. I know what it's like."

"Mom, please, I just ate dinner." If one bite of apple counted as dinner.

"If we can't find someplace bigger before Christmas, we'll need to make your room into a nursery. I know you're not home often, but I don't want you to feel like you can't visit." I could hear the shake in her voice as the shock started to wear off.

"Don't worry, Mom. I've been meaning to call and let you know I planned to stay here through the summer again. It would be stupid for you and Dad to look for another place just so I have a room to myself. I'll be graduating soon, and I have no idea where I'll get a job." The house they rented was a small two-bedroom Cape Cod at the end of a cul-de-sac. The backyard was fenced in. When I was a child, I'd had plenty of room to play in the summer, and it was within walking distance of the school where mom taught. It was also the ugliest house in the nice neighborhood, which meant it was affordable. "So, am I getting brothers or sisters?"

"Boys. Your father wanted to let it be a surprise, but I think I've had enough surprises this year. Honey, it's so good to hear from you. You're a much better adult than we are. I wasn't much older than you when I met your father." I could hear the sound of the old sofa and could picture mom leaning back into the lumpy green cushions.

"Do you need me to come home and help?" I was impressed that I managed to keep the hopefulness out of my voice. It would be so easy to run back home, even if it was just for the summer, rather than trying to face my problems here.

"I think it's time you lived it up and made up for lost time. Juliet, you have always been responsible. I spend more time worrying about you not enjoying your life than actually being worried you'll do something stupid."

Laying back against the mattress, I updated mom on everything that had been happening, minus the events of today's trifecta of doom. By the time we said goodbye, I was more than ready for some living it up.

I had two options. I could either spend all night worrying as I scoured the internet for jobs and scholarships while mulling over the fact that at twenty-one I was going to be getting siblings, which stopped any thoughts of retreating home. Or I could call my bestie and enjoy whatever free drinks my cleavage could get me.

Option two sounded much better to me.

2
MALFUNCTION

"Stop slouching," Mel muttered, jamming her elbow into my ribs.

"My drink is empty." I straightened, raising an eyebrow in challenge.

We'd made a deal before going out. I'd let her pick my outfit in exchange for her keeping a drink in my hand all night. I now had enough cheap vodka in my system to take away the insecurities over the clothes Mel had chosen.

"Be right back." She snorted before sashaying back to the bar.

I let my shoulders slump forward, looking down to realize that it didn't make the leather bralette Mel dressed me in any less revealing. Quite the opposite. With a sigh, I pulled my shoulders back, swaying to the beat.

"Screw it." I downed the rest of Mel's water and relinquished our sticky table to head for the dance floor as Sia sounded over the speakers. The wedges Mel picked for me tonight made me taller than most of the people on the dance floor, so I knew she wouldn't have any trouble finding me.

The liquor in my system, coupled with my love of dance, had the tension in my body unknotting itself. My shoulders relaxed. I gave into the bass thrumming around me, letting the last of my inhibitions go. I surrendered to the music, feeling wild and free. Why didn't I do this more often?

Maybe I was too old for my age?

A hand firmly grabs my breast, making my eyes snap open and breaking the spell of the booze and the music. The cool fingers against my skin made me feel equal parts shock and outrage as I wondered if tonight was going to end with my first bar fight. Was that the college rite of passage my mom had been talking about me missing out on?

Standing in front of me was Mel, her expression amused as she glanced down to show me she was upholding the girl code since my boob had decided to free itself.

Embarrassment burned as I looked to find more than a few gazes on me. Behind Mel was a guy who looked vaguely familiar. He at least had the decency to look away when I caught him staring.

Apparently, there was a thing as feeling too free, which my left tit had just proved.

"Maybe you were right about that top. Your face is so red right now." Mel snorted as I righted my wardrobe malfunction, swatting her hand away.

"I was definitely right." I mumbled as the song changed.

"Don't be embarrassed. You just made yourself more approachable."

Mel handed me a drink; the guy from earlier still stood behind her, keeping his gaze trained downward. Which was better than the leers I could see in my peripheral vision. I tilted my head to the side, trying to place where I knew him from, welcoming the distraction as the burn slowly eased from my face.

"Are you in my physiology class?" I called out to him. It was going to be a lot of fun going to class on Monday. Glancing around, I noticed a lot of semi-familiar faces. Perfect. How many saw my tit?

The guy cleared his throat. "I'm in Heeler's class. I sit a row behind you. I'm Noah."

"Noah was kind enough to buy our drinks." Mel gave me a knowing look.

"I'm here with some friends. We have a table in the back." Noah pointed toward the far corner. "There's extra room if you want to join us." The boyish grin he gave me took the edge off my lingering embarrassment. Bonus points for having a dimple. I remembered him from class because he always held the door. He was on the baseball team.

"He wants you." I swore Mel's eyes twinkled as she gave my boob a squeeze.

"He's a guy, and my boob was hanging out. Of course, he looks like he wants in my pants." I rolled my eyes. Unlike my best friend, I didn't need a guy between my legs to unwind. Not that I was judging. Mel had better luck finding talented bed partners than I did.

"Take your pick, Jules. Any of these guys could be yours for the night." She leaned in, moving her body against mine. Mel owned her sexuality in a way I never could There were plenty of times I'd cursed my chest while playing sports. A good sports bra was hard to find for a busty girl.

To humor her, I glanced around the dance floor, swaying to the music as I sipped my drink. Sure, there were plenty of attractive guys, and it had been months since my last hookup, which sadly had ended before the condom was fully on. Even I had felt bad for the guy.

"Noah keeps watching you." Mel had the gleam in her eye that always meant trouble.

"He's all yours." I wasn't wired for casual sex. It left me feeling let down. I needed a connection that went beyond the physical.

"You're hopeless." She rolled her eyes.

"No, I have a vibrator and nimble fingers." The music stopped, making my reply draw the attention of everyone standing nearby and causing my friend to laugh loudly enough to draw more attention our way.

Someone please kill me now. I was never going to be able to show my face here again.

"If you didn't before, now you have the interest of every guy around us." She laughed, but she wasn't wrong. I could see all the renewed interest coming our way. I wasn't willing to tempt fate with the way my day had been going to risk pregnancy or disease for, if I was lucky, what could be ten minutes of awkwardness.

"I keep telling you that if you actually found a guy who knew what he was doing, it would change your whole stance on casual sex." Scanning the dance floor, Mel pointed out a guy in jeans and a dark grey tee. "That one would be good. See the way he's moving his hips?" He was dry humping a girl on the dance floor. "Now, the dude in the stripes? He has no rhythm. You study how the body moves. I shouldn't have to point this out to you. Striped guy is all shoulders and zero movement below the waist. He would be all pump and dump. He's probably never made a woman come on purpose—or by accident, for that matter."

"As opposed to the humper?" I challenged, trying not to sound overly interested. I'd never thought of it that way before. "How do you know if he isn't just a good dancer? Maybe the other guy is nervous, or he hates dancing."

"Well, answer me this: who would you rather have on top of you? Mister shoulder wobble or the hip thruster?" Mel asked with a lick of her lips.

"When you put it that way…" I downed the rest of my drink and warmth pooled in my belly. I'd slept with six guys, not counting the premature condom-ejaculator. None had been anything to brag about. I had only seen two of them dance, and they'd both resembled the guy in the stripes. Was Mel on to something?

"Incoming," Mel whispered. "I told you he was interested."

I wanted to ask if she'd ever seen Noah dance. Maybe it was the vodka finally soaking through all the fatty carbs from my severance lasagna, but I was suddenly willing to test Mel's theory. In the name of science, of course.

"My girl, here, is kind of shy," Mel said to him. "I was want to make sure that she'd have some fun tonight because she's had a bad day. Would you like to help with that, Noah?" I couldn't help but roll my eyes at how easy it was for Mel to get guys to do what she wanted. Maybe that was another thing I should try. After all, she'd been right about my clothing. I would have to have been blind not to notice how much more attention had come my way when I'd worn something other than my usual jeans and hoodies.

"You're having a bad day, Juliet?" Noah turned his attention on me, looking sincere.

"It's the worst kind of day," Mel said, looking sad as she glanced my way. "I need to use the restroom, but I don't want to leave her alone, considering the last time I did she flashed the dance floor and caught the attention of every pervert in this place. Care to keep her company until I get

ACCIDENTAL P*RNSTAR

back?" Mel flashed her signature smile, which never failed to get her what she wanted.

"I'd be happy to." Noah stepped closer. "Has someone been bothering you?" Noah leaned in closer, his face losing the boyish charm to turn serious.

"Not really." I bit my lip because I was taken off guard by the change in his expression.

"I haven't seen you here before." Noah leaned down to speak into my ear. His hips moved in time with mine. As his hand gripped my hip, his fingers grazed my bare skin, pulling our bodies close just short of touching. "Is this okay?"

Thinking of what Mel had said about men and dancing, I nodded and closed the minute distance between us.

"I don't get out much. I'm a kinesiology major, minoring in sports medicine, so most of my time is spent studying or working. Or it was. I got fired today."

Noah nodded, and I leaned my body closer to his.

"That's rough. You worked at the Italian diner across from campus, right?" Noah asked, pulling my attention away from the fact he wasn't a terrible dancer. He easily synced his movements to my own.

"That was it," I said and Noah nodded again as we continued dancing.

"Are you seeing anyone?" he asked between songs.

"Nope." Shaking my head enough to sway my hair.

"I'm the same way. Between baseball and keeping up my grades, there isn't time for relationships. So, it's safe to assume I won't be making anyone jealous right now?"

"I wouldn't say that. I've been getting some intense side-eye from some other women." I sucked at flirting, but years of playing sports had taught me how to be good at friendly heckling. I was better at being one of the boys. Something Mel had tried hard to break.

"I was more worried about a boyfriend trying to make me leave you alone." Noah laughed, flashing that dimple again. "I assume guy trouble wasn't what caused your bad day."

Now, it was my turn to laugh. "I lost my job, my scholarship for summer, and next year, my roommate, who is a complete witch, meaning I need to find a new place to live. That, I can't afford, which means I'll probably end up in campus housing. I called my parents about commuting from home and found out I'm going to be a big sister. Plus, I flashed a bar full of people, and then loudly announced my love of masturbating to the same crowd." That thought was sobering. Hell, my current streak of bad luck was downright depressing.

"I missed that last one." Noah laughed and his chest brushed against mine. "I was expecting something…less. Like you forget to save a paper and your computer crashed, or maybe some guy didn't call you back. But you have definitely had a really bad day." Noah chuckled, letting his lips brush my ear. "A buddy of mine has a spare room. He's talked about renting it out, if you want to stay off campus. He's a good guy. We took a computer programming course together freshman year." Noah scanned the crowd before giving a triumphant fist pump. "He's still here, too. Come on, I'll introduce you." Winding his fingers through mine, he led me toward his friends.

"Mase, man, I have someone for you to meet," Noah said, talking over the noise around us as I scanned the bar for Mel, wondering where she'd disappeared to.

"Jules?" Even in a noisy room, I recognized that voice. Turning, I found myself looking at my former roommate, who was still looking as hot as ever.

Mason was the only man who'd ever caught me masturbating, so if I'd never seen him again I'd have been cool with it. It seemed fitting that I'd run into him today, of all days.

"Hey." Heat flooded my face as I looked anywhere but at that chiseled jaw that I'd never used for fapping inspiration, especially in the shower, where I might've forgotten to lock the door. That never happened.

"You two know each other?" Noah asked, standing close.

"Jules and I used to be roommates before I got my own place. How is Chelsea these days?"

I rolled my eyes. "Completely deranged and engaged to Ethan." Apparently, my anger at her was enough to break any lingering fap-related embarrassment.

"No shit?" Mason barked a loud laugh.

"Yep. She lectured me today because I didn't offer to pay more rent now that she doesn't feel right taking money from Ethan." I raised an eyebrow as Mason shook his head.

"So, Jules was just telling me about her bad day, and that she's looking for a new place to live. Are you still interested in renting your spare room?" Noah asked, his fingers still laced in mine. When I notice the way Mason's eyes linger there, I try to free my hand without drawing any attention.

"Maybe," he murmured. "Are you interested?"

I drew a deep breath. "After today, I wouldn't stay with Chelsea another semester even if she'd let me." Because as it was, I knew the next few weeks were going to suck. Chelsea was one to hold grudges. She'd be sure to make plenty of very loud trips up and down the stairs before I left.

Mason smirked. "You got on her bad side by refusing to pay more rent?"

"I'm not even sure she has a good side." One hard jerk, and my hand was free. I pretended not to notice the grin slipping from Noah's face.

Mason's gaze rose from my hand to lock with mine. "I'm getting ready to head home. If you want to come over, I'll give you a tour. You can see if you're interested."

"Afterparty at your house?" Noah's voice got the attention of the surrounding group.

"Did someone say party?" Mel sidled up, bumping my hip.

Mason just shrugged. "Do you two need a ride?"

Mason was watching me, but it was Mel who answered before I had time to think of all reasons why this was a bad idea. I was still trying not to dwell on my problems, and the alcohol in my system wasn't nearly enough to make me forget my day, or the fact that Mason had seen me two fingers deep, as Mel and I followed Mason out to his car. Except it wasn't the old dented and rusted Nissan he'd driven last year.

"Nice!" Mel says the exact thing I'm thinking as he hit a button on his key fob, making the lights of dark, two-door Lexus flash. "You can have shotgun, but you're going to owe me," Mel whispered as she climbed into the back.

The interior still had the smell of new car and leather. My car still smelled like the greasy burgers from my job at the burger shack in high school, mixed with the tomato sauce from Mama Rosa's.

How the hell could Mason afford this? Before fap-gate, we'd spent more than one night sharing ramen noodles.

"Are your classes still going okay?" Mason asked, pushing the button to start his car. My car didn't even have working keyless locks anymore.

"I have a couple of finals that are going to suck. I appreciate you offering to show me your apartment, but I'm probably not going to be able to afford the rent, even if it was the same as Chelsea charged. I got fired."

"Rosa fired you? What did you do, take the Lord's name in vain or break one of her son's hearts?" Mason laughed, seeming to find humor in the shittiness of my day.

"She gave my job to one of her nieces. I start jobhunting tomorrow." Watching the street lights pass by, I tried not to start feeling bad about myself.

"And she lost her scholarship," Mel added from the backseat. "Oh, and she's going to be a big sister."

"You're pregnant?" Mason's voice was just under a shout, and he jerked the car to the right.

"No, ass! When, in the very distant future I have kids, Jules will be an Auntie." Mel snorted from the backseat, adding a curse under her breath.

"So, Noah wasn't lying when he said you've had a bad day," Mason muttered.

When he flipped the turn indicator, I was shocked when he pulled up to a gated condo complex just a little north of campus.

3
SLIPPERY WHEN WET

"You live here? Did you win the lottery and not tell anyone?" Mel's mouth dropped open as she leaned between the seats.

I was thinking the same thing because this was the nice part of town. The part of town Chelsea's little townhouse bordered but wasn't actually in.

The car. The fancy apartment. Mason had either hit the lottery or had taken on a massive amount of debt. No wonder he wanted to rent his spare room.

Mel and I were both too stunned to do anything other than stare as he pulled into a garage and led us into his unit. It was the nicest house I'd ever been inside, and I knew that Mason's family didn't have money. So, how he managed to pay for this and tuition, I had no idea. The floors were tile and real wood, not the cheap-looking fake stuff peeling up in my parent's house. The counters in the kitchen were the white marble with grey veining that I'd always wanted in my kitchen when I got a house, someday.

"I've got to go buzz the guys past the gate to make sure they don't take the neighbor's parking spot. Make yourself at home." Mason slipped out the front door from an honest to God foyer. What college guy had a foyer?

"I think his condo is bigger than my parent's house," I utter, still completely in shock.

"This is insane. Tell me how if you like Noah because I think he was a little jealous we rode with Mason." Mel turned, heading back to the kitchen.

I groaned. "Noah is nice."

"He is a super nice guy and makes sure both parties enjoy their naked time together." Mel winked at me as she started opening cabinets. "Where do you think he keeps the booze? I don't want you losing your buzz."

"Wait, you're trying to set me up with someone you slept with? Isn't that against girl code? I don't want to have sex with your ex." I pulled out a stool and sat at the island in the middle of the kitchen. My feet were throbbing thanks to the heels.

"Noah isn't my ex. We hooked up freshman year. I know you haven't had any luck in the—" Mel started humping the air in front of her, making me laugh, "department. But I can guarantee you that Noah won't stop until you've had your happy ending. He's sweet. A little too boy-next-door for me, but he should be right up your alley—or could be if you let him."

"I really don't think I should chance being pregnancy buddies with my mom and given how everything today has gone so epically bad, I'm not going to chance it." I let my finger chase the grey veining on the white marble of the counter. The buzz had left the building.

"Bingo!" Mel jumped up and down while grabbing a bottle of vodka from a cabinet beside the fridge, and then plucked a bottle of orange juice from inside the fridge. "A screwdriver for milady."

"Mason seems interested. I know you think he is attractive." Mel smirked, opening a bottle of water and taking a drink just as the sound of the front door signaled, we were no longer alone.

"Hey," Mel plastered on her smile as Noah

came into the kitchen. "Want to show me the bathroom?" She gave me a wink as they passed Mason.

"She searched your kitchen until she found the booze." I shook my glass before taking a big drink and tried not to cough. Good vodka with a liberal pour packed a much bigger kick than what I'd been drinking before.

"Ready for a quick tour?" he asked. "I think the guys are going to play Xbox so that should keep them entertained for a bit."

"Sure, how have things been for you?" I asked taking another big drink, which must have been too much for my brain to coordinate because my shoe got caught and I ended up stumbling off the stool, spilling my drink like a lush.

Smooth, Jules. Smooth. What a waste of good booze.

"Careful, the tile is slippery when it gets wet." Mason just chuckled, and I tried to dazzle with a smile, wanting to play it off. Instead, I stepped in liquid and went down, my knee slamming into the hard tile at the same time my forehead hit something hard. I barked out a curse as Mason groaned above me. That's when I realize Mason tried to catch me and got a head butt to his crotch for his trouble.

"Oh, God," I bit out, trying not to panic when I

feel my hair stick on something. "Are you wearing a belt?" I wheezed, trying to rise up, only to feel a sharp tug on my scalp as I tumbled back into his crotch. "Oh, my God," I muttered feeling the need to completely freak out as Mason's hands on my shoulders gave me a slight squeeze.

"Please, stop moving." His voice was tight, making my face heat as I realized my face is in his crotch. Nose to balls.

Holy shit.

"Okay." Taking a deep breath, I steadied myself by putting my hands on his thighs. "My hair is stuck."

"Give me a minute to recover." Mason was still wheezing, and I recognized he was trying to stay still and not pull my hair.

"Just let me get your belt off so I can stand up." Moving my hands up his thighs, I felt a bulge at his zipper, which was situated right at eye level. "Or I can just wait a minute." I dropped my hands, trying and failing not to stare at his dick. "Ow. Ow. Careful." I could feel Mason fumbling with his belt, pulling at my hair. I was sure I'd have a bald spot before I was free.

"You're bleeding," Mason said once I was on my feet.

Then I felt a burning on my forehead.

"I have a first aid kit. Follow me."

As I walked out of the kitchen, I noticed the three guys on the couch, plus Mel, all silently staring as we walked past the doorway to the living room.

4
BIG SAUSAGE

It felt like someone was jumping on the bed, making my head and stomach protest as I burrowed deeper into the blankets.

"Bitch, you made me swear on our friendship I wouldn't let you sleep in today no matter how much you whined and begged." Mel laughed and another mini-earthquake shook the bed as she jumped up and down on the mattress.

"Ugh." I mumbled and tightened my hold on the pillow over my head.

"You have to find a job today, remember? And because I rock, I got you the college hangover survival kit." Mel jerked away the pillow from my head and I caught a whiff of bacon.

"Is it a bacon and cheese croissant from

Schmidt's, with extra bacon?" I popped open my eyes, feeling hopeful even as my head ached.

"And a blue sports drink with Tylenol on the side." She started shaking the bed again.

"I'm up. I'm up." Slowly, I sat up, thankful my stomach wasn't protesting as she tossed a white paper sack in my lap. The smell made my mouth water.

"I'm pretty sure you got all your puking out before we got home, so you should be good to go today." Mel laughed.

"I puked?" My words are distorted by my full mouth.

"You don't remember last night at all, do you?" Mel, still laughing, fell back on the bed.

I paused, the sandwich halfway to my mouth. "We went to the shitty little bar by campus." I strained to think what had happened next because I remembered being somewhere else. "Then we went to Noah's house?"

"Mason's. We went to Mason's house. You had more chemistry with him than Noah, so I distracted Noah while you apparently blew Mason in his kitchen."

"What? I did not!" I'm shocked enough to drop

the sandwich, but then I recalled a flash of being on my knees.

"You didn't. But the guys think you did. You fell, and in a move only you could pull off, got your hair stuck. Jack went into the kitchen and saw just enough to come back and tell us all you were giving Mason a blowjob. Then you two disappeared into his bathroom. Like any good friend, I checked even though it meant I could've totally been cock-blocking you. Your forehead hit his belt buckle, and Mason was kind enough to offer a first aid kit."

"So, everyone figured out I didn't really do that in a kitchen with a bunch of people in the next room, right?" My sandwich was completely forgotten.

"I'm sure Mason will tell them nothing happened if they ask him." Mel picked at her nails, which was the only tell she had.

"Why didn't he tell them last night?" I asked, picking up my sandwich again.

"Well, once your head was bandaged, you realized you had spilled the rest of your drink in your lap, and you thought that was hilarious." She grinned. "You complained it was sticky, so you took off my shoes and decided you were going to take a shower. You proved that vodka is not your friend. " Mel paused to look at me.

"That doesn't sound bad, so what's with the dramatic pauses?" I took another bite of my sandwich, knowing I needed to eat and hydrate to function today. She was right, vodka always hit me hard.

"You didn't wait for me or Mason to leave the bathroom before you stripped down to your birthday suit, and kudos by the way, you have a rocking body. In case you were wondering, Mason couldn't keep his eyes offf you. Anyway, he let you borrow some clothes and asked me to make sure you didn't slip in the shower."

"I got naked in front you and Mason?" A piece of semi-chewed bacon flew out of my mouth, making Mel grimace.

"You started talking about how hot you thought he was, asking if he remembered the last time he caught you in the shower? I never realized you were such a dirty talker. You have been holding out on me. Anyway, by the time we got you dressed—"

"Mason helped me get dressed?" I screeched, my voice rising an octave.

"He lingered in his bedroom in case I needed any help with you. Apparently, he hasn't seen you drunk before. You weren't that bad. That first

Halloween frat party was worse." The party she was talking about had been the first party I'd gone to. We'd both gotten drunk and picked up by campus police for puking in the bushes on the way back to our dorm.

"With the way you always complained about him, I expected Mason to be a douche, but he was actually very nice. He tossed your clothes in the washer and dried them." It's only now that I realized I was still wearing a guy's shirt. "His shorts were too big for you, so you ran around in just his shirt last night, and let me tell you, I've seen more of your ass and vajayjay than I ever intended to—which have you ever thought about waxing? It's getting a little wild down there."

"Shut up. I was flashing a bunch of guys?" This was why I didn't drink much. Jules without inhibitions was crazy with no shame.

"Well, no. By the time you were as dressed as you decided to get, the guys had already left. I think Mason kicked everyone out so they wouldn't see your naughty bits. Noah has texted me a few times this morning, but I wasn't sure what you wanted me to tell him so I haven't responded."

"And how did we get back here?" I asked in a little voice.

"Mason brought us. Don't worry, you didn't puke until you got back here, and I think it's because you switched from vodka to beer."

"I hate beer. Why would I drink beer?"

"I think you were trying to flirt."

I felt my face burn as I closed my eyes.

"Then you told him how hot you thought he was. Again. Even drunk, you suck at flirting—just so you know. Then you did a cartwheel, flashed us your business, and I figured I needed to get you the hell out of there."

Keeping my eyes closed, I finished my sandwich. Then swallowing hard to get down one last huge bite, because I wanted this conversation over, I opened my eyes. "Okay, well, it sounds like a really fun night. But I do have things to do today." I finished my drink and scooted to the edge of the bed.

"Are you really going to move into Mason's spare room?" Mel asked.

"I can't keep living at Chelsea's. My lease is only good until the end of the month. I can't check about campus housing over the summer until Monday, and hopefully by then, I'll have another job. I know I can't afford whatever he wants." Details of our conversation were hazy but slowly trickling in. I remembered how nice his place had been. How good his car had smelled.

"I can't move back home. Mom and Dad plan on using my room as the nursery. If I go back over the summer, they'll think they need to find a bigger place they can't afford." Mom claimed to be looking for a bigger place, but I didn't need to want kids to know that babies were expensive. They didn't need the stress of me coming home. "I have a few weeks to think of something." Standing up, I realize I'm still wearing Mason's shirt and a pair of basketball shorts cinched at my waist.

"I insisted you wear pants home." She laughed again. "I forgot how much fun you can be when you let yourself loose. Feel free to raid my closet, but you do realize at some point you're going to have to see him again and get the clothes we left behind. That top was one of my favorites, so if you're thinking of leaving them there, I'm not going to let you."

"If it's your favorite, you go get it," I whined. Then I started going through her clothes until I found a pair of jeans and a top that looked nice enough to job hunt in without being too casual or too revealing before using her ensuite shower.

. . .

I spent all afternoon putting in my applications everywhere within walking distance of campus. Most places weren't hiring, but I did find an all-night diner that was looking for a waitress to work the third shift. It wasn't the best option, but if they called me back, I'd take it.

I'd also snagged a free campus newspaper to browse rental listings, but anything in my possible budget was going to make a walking commute hard. Not to mention I wasn't exactly planning on walking back and forth to work at four AM.

By the time I saw my trusty rusty car parked on the curb in front of Chelsea's house, I was ready to admit defeat. The hangover was not helping my resolve. Student loans for my last year of college wouldn't be the end of the world. I went over what I still had in savings, and if I didn't take summer classes, I could afford to rent a place in town, but I'd be sleeping on the floor and eating from whatever utensils I could pick up at the dollar store. Totally doable, but not an ideal situation since it would drain my savings and mean that I would either have to double my class load next year or not graduate on time.

More classes meant less time to work on keeping

my GPA up. Plus, next year, I would need clinical hours, which was going to cut into work time.

Sighing in frustration, I came up short when I noticed the sleek coupe parked in the driveway. The temptation to keep walking was almost enough to help me forget my growling stomach.

Unlocking the front door as quietly as possible, I ignored the voices coming from the living room and sneaked into the kitchen. My plan was to grab a yogurt and some granola and fruit and retreat to my little sanctuary under the stairs. Once I opened the fridge, I realized that wasn't going to happen.

My food was gone. Not just someone snagged a yogurt or a premade salad, which would have been annoying, but I'd live. Every single thing I'd bought, including the cartoon of eggs and salad dressing, was gone. In their place were neatly organized foods labeled with Chelsea and Ethan's name.

The bowl of fruit that I kept stocked on the counter was also missing. I felt my annoyance turn into anger as I debated my options. I could pull out my phone and place an order for delivery. I could go into the living room and drag Chelsea around by her hair or walk back to campus and grab something from the student union.

I went with option four. Opening the fridge, I

grabbed a Diet Coke and a container, not really caring what was in it. Then I enter the living room.

"What's up?" I gave a head bob to Mason as I flopped down on the couch beside Chelsea.

"What are you doing?" Her voice got higher as she spoke. "That's my food, Jules." Her smile was sweet as her eyes flicked to Mason like she was afraid I'd embarrass her in front of company. As if Mason wasn't already aware of her brand of crazy.

"Well, Chelsea," I said, airily, "seeing as how all of my food is gone and I've had a long day and it's dinner time, I'm eating." For effect, I opened the lid on the chicken and broccoli and used my fingers to pop a piece in my mouth.

"I cleaned out kitchen today and threw out all the bad food."

"And apparently unexpired yogurt and fresh fruit are bad? Funny how only my food is gone?" I popped another piece of food in my mouth, using my fingers and being sure to be messy about it.

"If you're going to act like a child about this, I'm happy to share my food with you until you get to the store." Chelsea turned her attention back to Mason. "So, Ethan told me you've been coding for a big company based in California. That's got to be exciting. Is it just an internship?"

I could practically hear the cha-ching sounding in her mind. Chelsea was nothing if not greedy.

"It's freelance, for now. After graduation, I'm hoping to land a fulltime position." Mason watched me with a smirk as I opened the little can of pop and took a big drink. Everyone in this room knew I hated diet soda. Maybe I was being childish, but no one had ever said I was perfect, and I needed something to get the gross taste of Chelsea's cooking out of my mouth.

"Jules, I came by since we really didn't get a chance to finish our talk last night." His voice made heat flood my cheeks. "Want to grab dinner?"

"You were with Mason last night?" Chelsea asked, but I was ignoring her and got to my feet.

"Sure." I was on my feet and putting the uneaten food in the trash before I realized Mason was following me.

"Has today gone any better for you?" he asked with a grin then laughed when I shrugged him off.

"Let me grab my keys." I head to my room and grab my purse and keys being sure to grab the clothes I'd borrowed last night. "Do you want me to wash these before I give them back?" I held up the clothes and Mason just shrugged.

"I'll drive so you don't risk losing your precious

parking spot." Mason gave me a grin. And I just went with it because I was happy to save on gas.

His car was even nicer in the daytime. We decided to order pizza and have it delivered to his place so he could show me the spare room and give me another tour since my memory from last night was, thankfully, still spotty enough I had plausible deniability.

And my secret crush confession? Where in the hell had that come from? Mason was hot and nice but anyone could see that.

"I know you said you were looking for a job, and I'm not really hard up for money, so if you're interested, I'll float you until you have a job as long as you promise to cook dinner." Mason was showing me through his condo that looked even nicer with sober eyes. "And after, I'll charge the same that you're paying Chelsea if that works for you."

"What's the catch?" Because I'd lived with Mason for almost a year and hadn't found any defects that would make me question his sanity, and this deal he was offering seemed too good to be true. Mason wasn't duplicitous.

"My work schedule is a little different, and I don't let people in my home office. You can park in the spare spot in the garage." I followed Mason down a hall that seemed vaguely familiar. "This is my master suite. This is my office." I followed Mason down a hall that seemed vaguely familiar as he pointed to doors on. "This is the spare bathroom you would use. That last door is your room." He hesitated drawing my attention back to him. "My work schedule is a little different. I keep my office door locked because I don't want people in there." Another pause. "You can park in the spare spot in the garage. We never had problems with sharing the kitchen and living room at Chelsea's so I don't think that would be a problem."

I nod as we stop in front of the Mason called mine.

It was an actual bedroom. Bigger than my room back home. Bigger than my parents' bedroom. The walls were a soft grey, and the floor was dark wood. There was a queen-size bed with white bedding and a grey tufted headboard. A small nightstand and a large dresser were the only other furniture in the room.

"How do you afford this?" I gaped because I couldn't make sense of it. Mason fidgeted, looking everywhere but at me, and for the first time since I'd known him, he seemed unsure of himself.

"That has to do with the other thing I wanted to talk to you about." He shoved his hands in his pockets, and I waited for the punchline, although I'm not sure I really wanted to know.

"You're not into anything illegal…?"

He tilted his hand back and laughed. "It's not illegal. It's just something I haven't told anyone about, so I'm really trusting you with this."

"Is this a 'once I tell you I'll have to kill you' type of thing?" I joked.

"Follow me." Mason led me to the door he'd pointed out for his office. "So, I do code for a company based out West. But I also do other work for that company." The office looked a lot like the bedroom we were just in except the headboard is a dark wood, and there's a brown leather bucket chair in the corner. The walls were off white with a beige carpet over the floors, and it looked generic, impersonal. A massive desk with computer monitors and a camera sat across from the bed. "I'm just going to show you and hope that you understand this isn't something I want spread around. I'm not ashamed of it, but I value my privacy, and most people aren't very open-minded. You've always been cool. Not catty or petty like Chelsea. Not into gossip like Mel."

I wanted to defend my best friend, but what was the point in arguing with the truth? She did love juicy gossip.

Mason went to the computer, and after hitting a few keys, played a video that was taken in this room. A video of a man, naked from the neck down, sitting in a chair that looked familiar. Looking over my shoulder and back at the screen, I confirmed what my mind was telling me as I watched the man start jacking off. It took another minute for things to click into place.

"Oh!" My mouth fell open, and I knew I should've turned around, but part of me was fascinated by what I was seeing. The rest of me wasn't sure what to think. "That's you. Oh, shit. That's you." Heat floods my entire body. Mason's dick was nice. Long and thick, with well-defined tip, and I needed to stop staring because I was ready to drool. "So, I guess we're even." I wanted to look back at the screen and fought a losing battle. Mason was hung. I think Mel might have had the right idea about me losing my inhibitions and letting sex temporarily solve my problems. Not that I planned to tell her that. My best friend would be insufferable.

"The company I work for is called Allfans. I do

coding and troubleshooting, but the site is subscription-based and allows creators to charge people to view their content. This is some of mine." Mason talked, but I still didn't turn around. My face felt like it was on fire, and I wasn't sure how to look at him without thinking about his dick now. Or the fact that he'd seen me naked. Oh shit, I was watching him naked right now, doing something that was making my thighs clench.

When the doorbell rang, I couldn't get to the kitchen fast enough. I was debating on whether to try my luck at the stool again when Mason set the pizza down on the center island.

"So, it pays well?" I asked him, my gaze darting around the kitchen. This place suddenly made more sense.

"It was slow at first, but in the last year, I really developed a following and have gotten a better percentage. I'm in the top five most downloaded for six months straight, so I started doing requests and a few live shows, which gives me a higher percentage." His face flushed, but he turned to the fridge, grabbing two bottles of water.

I grabbed a slice of pizza and chewed while I mulled over what he was telling me. I couldn't lie and say I'd never seen porn. After the brief clip I'd seen, I got why he was so popular. I'd seen Mason without a shirt before, so I already knew he was built. I just hadn't realized he was hung.

I had limited experience with men and sex. None of my partners had been as big as Mason. Which I had liked about Jacob when he'd punched my V-card after prom. It had still hurt, but I was pretty sure Mason would've destroyed my vagina, not just my hymen.

"You're quiet," Mason said, and I realized he was waiting for some kind of reaction from me.

"It's impressive you're able to afford the rent on this place plus your car. I'm not going to judge you."

"Um, I don't rent this place. I bought it. It was an older unit that needed updating, so I got a decent deal and did as much work as I could myself."

My jaw dropped. "You own this?" Mason was my age and already owned more property than my own parents did.

"I figured it would be a good investment. I can lease it out if I decide not to stay in the area or sell it outright. I own the Lexus, too. I spent a little more than I probably should have, but I'm a guy. I can't make all responsible financial decisions."

Mason didn't sound conceited or bragging. He was just stating facts.

"Holy shit. And you're taking out loans for school?" Because no way was he jacking off making this kind of money. I'd been doing it for years without making a cent.

"I have enough put back to pay for my last year. I've already paid off the loan I took out. Once my 401k hits my goal, I'll stop releasing new videos. After that, there could be residual income from the videos, but I'll be fine without." Mason was eating a slice of pizza while I let mine hang halfway to my mouth.

"And all you do is masturbate and let people watch the videos?"

"I've done live sessions with a mask, and I post photos just to keep switching things up." Mason was tossing looks my way, looking a little hesitant. "I always keep my face hidden. I think it's part of my success."

"Wow. I just spent all afternoon trying to find a job that will pay me just a little more than minimum wage, so I won't have to take out as many student loans for next year. I'm kind of jealous you don't have to worry about tuition."

Mason had a retirement account. I had just over

a thousand dollars in savings and an emergency stash of fifty hidden in a tampon box. My car was barely worth scrap price, and my laptop was the most expensive thing I owned. I'd found a good deal on a refurbished model and was lucky it was lasting.

"I have been getting a lot of requests for videos with a partner." Again, Mason looks hesitant. "More than a few sponsor offers as well."

I blinked. "I mean, it wouldn't really be any different from living in a dorm or any situation with roommates, right? Only you're getting paid good money for bumping uglies. That doesn't bother me if that is what you're worried about." Chelsea and Ethan caused me to splurge on noise-cancelling headphones.

"So, you'll do it?" Mason seemed relieved.

"I'd be kind of stupid to pass up a chance to not have to live in campus housing this summer." I took a big bite of pizza.

"I wasn't sure you'd go for it. You're fun but seem to always keep yourself on a tight leash. We've always gotten along. Last night proved we have great chemistry. We should probably set some loose ground rules…?"

I nod so Mason continues.

"This would be entirely up to you, but I should hit my retirement savings goal by graduation. I think it would be too complicated to try to start a relationship while I'm still posting—especially if I'm going to post videos with a partner."

I nod again.

"I'm not really sure what will come of things, but I thought we could just split the amount offered. I have more than one request, so you could look them over and see what you'd be comfortable with. We could do as many or as few as you're interested in. If you decide to set up your own channel, I could help with that. Or we could do a partnered one, which would make it easier to separate earnings that way."

"With me? Wait—" A piece of sausage flew out of my mouth, and I vowed right then to listen to all the times mom told me not to talk with my mouth full. "I thought you wanted to be sure I'm okay living here while you shoot porn videos down the hall. You want to do them with me?"

Mason wanted to fuck me? My stomach did a loop de loop, making my thighs clench.

5

THE DIFFERENCE IS YOU TAPE IT

"I want you to film with me." Mason just watched me as I chewed the food in my mouth. "I've been getting special requests for a while, but I hadn't considered taking them until now. I think five thousand is pretty motivating as well."

"You want to pay me twenty-five hundred to film us having sex?" I blurted after swallowing. That was more than I was used to making in a month.

"Five thousand would be *your* cut. The highest offer is ten," Mason clarified, and my ears started to ring as I gripped the countertop for support.

"Isn't that the same as prostitution?" I was considering this. I mean, I'd been thinking about sleeping with Mason since before seeing that video, but now, I couldn't stop thinking about it. Would mixing business and pleasure be a train wreck? If I moved in and we had sex, that would be awkward enough. Would it be any worse than him seeing me naked? Which had happened twice now.

"Trust me it's all legal. We could do the request on my channel, and then set up one for shared content if you decide you want to continue." Mason wasn't touching his food anymore and neither was I.

"I can't even do karaoke." I wasn't great under pressure in public. "I'm really not—"

"You were doing pants-less cartwheels in my living room last night after stripping down in front of your best friend and me."

"I was drunk!" It was easier not to think about all the repercussions of my actions when I was drinking. It's why I didn't do it very often. Although, if I could make five grand for one night of sex, it would help things a lot. I'd had bad sex for free. I doubted sex with Mason would be bad. Even just thinking of that video brought out my inner vixen.

"You can't be drunk or under the influence of any narcotics in any videos submitted. It violates their terms of service, and I don't want you to do anything you wouldn't be comfortable enough to do sober. I know that's what you were thinking." Mason sighed. "Listen, I'm not going to pressure you. The room is yours if you want it. Everything else is also your decision, but I understand if it's not something you'd be comfortable with. I hope you'll respect my privacy no matter what you decide."

"Absolutely. It's definitely a lot to think about." Which wasn't a lie. "You own your own home." Maybe that wasn't the biggest takeaway from tonight's conversation considering I'd seen a video of his dick about twenty minutes ago, but to me this house was mindboggling. I wanted to own my own place someday. Have stability and financial security. Not have to scrape to get by for my entire life until the daily grind killed me—that was the cycle my parents were stuck in.

"Why ask me?" Yeah, I worked out. Yoga, running, weights. However, I wasn't a fitness model by any means. I loved dairy and chocolate too much. If I really tried and took the time with my hair and makeup, I even impressed myself. Most days, I was too lazy to care.

"Like I said, I value my privacy. I'm not ashamed of how I'm making a living, but someday my wife or kids might suffer because of other people's closed mindedness. I know you well enough to know that you don't gossip. You hate drama and are probably as private a person as I am." Mason started clearing away our trash. "Do you want to stick around for a bit, or should I take you back to Chelsea's?"

I grimaced knowing that my taking the low road earlier was about to bite me in the ass.

"Do you care if we stop by the store on the way home? I need to pick up a few things." Even though Mason's place was about fifteen minutes north of campus, it was like living in a different world. His block had two different whole food stores, plus a Target, which was a win for me.

So, I wasn't completely dreading walking into my little closet under the stairs until I clicked the light on. Thrown on my bed was the food I'd stolen earlier and the mini can of diet pop. My stomach sank because I'd left my laptop open, and sure enough the keys and screen were a mess with sticky cancer-causing diet soda and bits of soy-covered broccoli and chicken.

I pulled out my phone to google the safest way to clean a computer then swallowed the building aggravation when my phone didn't connect to the Wi-Fi. Forcing myself to take a deep breath, I went in search of Chelsea, telling myself a criminal record would wreck any chances of landing a good job later.

"Where is Chelsea?"

Ethan barely pulled his gaze away from the TV.

"She went out earlier."

"Do you know why someone threw food all over my room and my computer?"

Ethan looked my way long enough to just show a little shock but no surprise. We both knew who'd done it.

"Is it ruined?" he asked, making my stomach plummet. I couldn't afford to replace it or get it fixed if it was something major. I had to have a computer for classes.

"I tried getting online but the Wi-Fi is down."

"It's not down. She changed the password." Ethan for once looked embarrassed by his bride-to-be's behavior. "It's 'Julesistrash.' Sorry. She was pretty pissy. You know how she can get."

I could feel my eyes burning but refused to cry. I could yell and scream all I wanted, but it wasn't going to change anything.

"Do you want me to take a look at it for you?" Ethan stood, but I shook my head.

It was a very sad thing that all of my possessions fit easily in the back of my car. It only took twenty minutes of furious activity to pack everything.

I was all packed up with nowhere to go.

Mel had offered her couch to me, but it wouldn't be a permanent solution, and I didn't want to make our friendship weird. Sometimes, Mel was cagey about her personal life, and I knew she hated sharing her living space. She said it came from growing up the oldest kid in a big family. Nothing had ever been hers.

Mason had said the room was mine, whether I wanted to make the video with him or not. I'd always gotten along with him.

"So, when you say that you value your privacy, you mean that no one who watches the videos know it's you?" I didn't offer any other greeting when Mason answered his phone. I'm still more than a little pissed off, and it's making me a little more reckless because, when I walked into my new room tonight, there was no way I was going to turn down Mason's offer.

"That's why I keep my office locked and tell people it's off-limits because of work. No one sees what it looks like. I make sure everything is edited so my face doesn't show unless I'm wearing a mask."

"I already paid Chelsea for this month and until I find another job, I can't afford to pay you too, but I'm willing to cook and clean up after myself. I'm also sitting outside the main gate, and the parking attendant is giving me the squirrelly-eye, so if you changed your mind about letting me stay—" The gate swung open before I could finish the sentence. Mason directed me to his unit and was waiting in the garage when I pulled up.

"So, I take it things didn't go well?" Mason asked, looking at the sadly empty backseat of my car.

"I don't really want to talk about it." I grab the bags in the passenger seat. The one with my food and the other with some clothes and my toiletries.

"About the other thing—" I came up short when Mason took the bags out of my hands.

"What else do you want to bring in?" Mason was looking at my backseat, and I felt out of place standing next to my POS car parked next to his. My car's value was probably less than his tires, and suddenly I felt really old and wary. And with that feeling came an understanding of what my mom and Mel had been talking about.

I hadn't been living. I'd been working. Probably too hard, and I hadn't seen how much I'd missed out on.

"This is all for tonight." I didn't even want to look at my computer. That problem would still be waiting for me tomorrow.

I cleared my throat. "About the other thing… I'm interested. I mean, I have a few questions and concerns. But you said five grand, right? For just one video. And no one will know it's either of us." I can't even begin to believe I'm saying it. But I'd thought a lot about it on the way over. More, I thought about the money. It would give me some breathing room. It wasn't going to cover the fall semester, but it would let me take classes this summer, which meant I could keep on track to graduate early. And loans to cover one year of college? That would be nothing. Sure, I'd have to pray my trusty rusty car held out for a few more years.

What was another awkward sexual encounter to add to my repertoire? Deep down, I didn't think anything with Mason would be awkward. I would be lying if I denied I'd always been attracted to

Mason. He was funny, smart, and sexy. If I was looking for a man to check all the boxes, it was him.

"It doesn't bother you to get paid for it?" I asked, following Mason through his apartment.

"Honestly, it was a little weird at first, but then I figured if I could get paid to do something I was already doing, why not? It beat spending my twenties killing myself to afford an education and feed myself."

Which were almost my exact sentiments.

"There's still pizza left if you get hungry. Help yourself to whatever is in the kitchen. I've got some reading to do for class next week but come find me if you need anything." Mason left me in my new-for-now room.

I pulled out my phone to see if Mel had texted me back yet. I'd given her a very abridged version to let her know I'd taken Mason up on his offer to live with him—but left out the porn parts.

Her response was an eggplant emoji.

If she only knew.

I wasn't sure if I wanted to talk terms just yet. I flopped back on the bed and felt like I was sitting on a cloud. Pulling out my phone, I pulled up the website Mason had talked about earlier.

I'd watched porn before but not solo porn. I

browsed around, wishing I knew Mason's username to pull up his profile. Mason had a great body. I'd never thought watching a guy masturbate would be hot, but I couldn't stop thinking about him.

I had just unpacked my vibrator, deciding the stressful day had more than earned me an orgasm, when a knock sounded on my door. My cheeks heated as I stashed my battery-operated-boyfriend under the pillows and told Mason the door was open.

"I forgot to mention the Wi-Fi passwords," he said, entering. "I use a VPN to keep the network secure, and the server I use for streaming is hard wired just to be safe, but this is the password and my login credentials for Allfans, so you can get a feel for the site." Mason set the stack on the dresser and lingered awkwardly at the door. "It's nice having someone else here. Sometimes, the quiet gets to be lonely."

Mason left before I could decipher his words. My attention was still stuck on the paper he'd left behind.

I'd had sex before. Only gotten oral once. Kyle went down on me during my sophomore year, but I was pretty sure treating it like chewing gum wasn't a proper technique.

But the thought of that experience wasn't what had me reaching under the pillow.

I logged into Wi-Fi and pulled up Mason's Allfans account, telling myself I needed to subscribe and do a little research.

6
BURST YOUR BUBBLE

"I'm proud you're taking the plunge to get waxed. I gotta say you were rocking quite the porno bush down there." Mel's voice carried as she held open the door to the salon.

"I shave." Sometimes. "It's not that bad."

Mel snorted. "Well, I don't think Mason minded at all, but I still think this is a good call." Mel stayed on my heels as I signed in with the receptionist. "The first time can be a little crazy. It's better to have a few times under your belt before anyone sees."

In the two weeks I'd been staying at Mason's, she'd been grilling me for details of which I had none. It isn't like I could tell her I was planning to fund my last year of school with sex. Not that I thought she would judge me. I knew Mel would accept it, probably even applaud it, but it wasn't just my secret. Still, keeping something from Mel didn't sit well.

I operated under the moral motto of, "If it's something you have to hide, it's not something you should be doing." This fell into a gray area.

Desperate times called for desperate measures, and I would be lying if the thought of spending some naked time with Mason didn't excite me. The deal Mason was offering seemed perfect.

A business arrangement.

Sure, if things got awkward, I'd still have to see him every day, but he'd already seen me masturbate and act like a drunken dumbass, so I figured I didn't have much else to lose.

"Do you like working at the diner?" Mel's voice drew my attention.

"It's nice. I make about the same in tips." The hours were flexible, too, because the owner was willing to work with my school schedule and was understanding of my need for sleep to function.

"Noah has been asking about you." Mel's mouth curled up into a wicked grin. "Apparently,

Mason came clean about the kitchen incident, but Noah got the feeling his interest in you wasn't very welcome."

"I doubt Mason cares either way. We're just roommates." I felt butterflies in my stomach as I tried to think about anything other than the fact hot wax was going to be introduced to my vagina and butthole soon.

"And you don't care either way. You just out of the blue decided to get everything waxed?"

Inwardly, I cringed. Mel knew me well enough to call my bullshit, and I already hate lying. "I'm taking your advice and mom's. I'm young and have been taking life way too seriously. It's time for me to start living my life." It wasn't a lie, exactly. "Staying at Mason's means I don't have to stress about housing. Starting at the diner so soon means my savings can stay put. I can use financial aid for tuition, which isn't ideal, but it isn't the end of the world. I only have a year left of school, and I plan to enjoy it."

"I am going to having you living it up until we graduate!" Mel hoots, drawing the attention of everyone which made me sink lower in my chair just as my name gets called.

"I'm Callie. This is your first time?" Callie was probably my mom's age but way more chipper than I could ever hope to be.

"Yes." I tossed one last look over my shoulder to Mel who gave me a thumbs up before giving the door a longing look.

"I like your shirt by the way." Callie giggled, and it made her seem more my age than the lines on her face and grey hairs let on.

"Thanks, I wore it special for today." Because I'd figured what would be better to wear to my first Brazilian than a Wookie shirt?

"Don't worry. Just relax, and let me do all the work. I'm going to give you a minute to get undressed and get on the table and lay on your back."

The door clicked shut as I kicked off my shoes and pulled down my yoga pants. I opted for the kick-and-flip over bending to pick my pants up. I mean, why not? Plus, there was something unsettling about being bent over and naked where anyone might happen by. It was bad enough I was getting hair ripped from places I'd rather not know I had hair.

After climbing on the table, I tried to find a

place to lay that didn't make me feel like a total weirdo, and by the time Callie was back in the room, I gave up. There was no way to feel relaxed with a stranger in your business.

"Doing this as a surprise for your boyfriend or girlfriend?" Callie started talking, but all I could focus on were the sounds of what I imagined was some sort of prep for torture.

"No, I just thought I'd try it out. You know, see what all the kids were talking about."

Callie laughed, and the sound was loud enough I was sure the entire place could hear, as she began slathering warm wax.

"I like people with a good sense of humor." Callie must also have liked torture because without any warning the first strip is ripped off, and I struggled not to let out a stream of curses at the woman who was still chuckling.

"This will be easier if you have fun with it." She laughed again, and now I was sure she was some kind of fetishist who liked the pain of others. "I've got some new dyes in if you want to try bleaching what's left and go for a wild color." She nodded toward the far corner.

"People actually dye something in that area

green? Isn't the point to attract people downtown, not send them running?" Green wasn't a color I'd associate with sexiness down there.

Callie chuckled again, ripping another strip away. "I never got that either, but different strokes for different folks." Callie's voice sounded distant as I tried to ignore the pain building in my crotch. Gritting my teeth, I gained a new respect for Mel who the lady balls to have this done regularly.

"Yea. Different strokes," I mumble, hoping that maybe if I kept her happy it might minimize the pain.

"Just a few more, and we'll turn you over."

I'm seriously considering nixing the full wax I'd signed on for. The back door had been no man's land, so maybe leaving a bit of hair there would be a good thing. It could be a groin mullet—party in the front-not entrance in the back style.

"Argh!" A few things happened once the next strip was ripped away. I thought maybe I was missing a part of my vagina.

"That's going to leave a mark." With wide eyes, I watch as she rubbed her jaw, and only then did I realize I'd kicked her.

"I'm sorry." Holy shit, I'd just kicked the woman responsible for handling my lady bits.

"Don't worry about it. It's happened before." Callie continued rubbing her jaw, and I suddenly had flashes of Rocky and Drago as she went back to the cart. "I told you I've seen it all. I just wasn't expecting it." She chuckled, making me wonder if I'd gotten the one waxer with a few screws lose. "That was it for the front. Time for the butt strip. Don't worry, I'll watch out for your feet of fury."

Once I rolled onto my stomach, I regretted honoring taco Tuesday this afternoon.

"I need you to hold your cheeks for me, and I'll make this quick."

"Um, maybe we could just skip this part." I tried to ignore the cool air hitting my butt, but the ridiculousness of the situation made me wonder if this was some huge joke. People did this regularly?

"Nonsense, I'm not going to let you regret your first wax because of some twitch. Trust me, the worst part is over."

I doubted it, but I was ready to go all in.

I shouldn't have. Warm wax being slathered between my cheeks was jarring enough without my digestive tract deciding to up the ante. The pop made me think of bubble gum. I willed myself to sink into the bed.

"Well, that was a new one," Callie mutters.

"Callie?" I murmured. "Please, just finish, and if you don't say anything else, I'll add a twenty to your tip." I was never coming back here. Ever. There was no way in hell I was ever living down the fact that I'd blown a wax bubble out of my ass.

7
THAT WAS QUICK

Days passed in a blur as finals neared and I settled into a new routine. I found a new waxer, one who had a thick Russian accent and who terrified me. I was pretty sure she could pummel me without breaking a sweat, a thought that made me feel confident future wax trips would happen without incident.

Mason had been laid back. We'd had one short conversation when he'd given me a copy of medical records showing he was clean. I'd made my own appointment at the student health center. I'd been on birth control since high school, it had been an embarrassing sixteenth birthday when my mom wanted to be sure I could be sexually active without an unplanned pregnancy. I wanted to show Mason the same respect he had given me. My results came in today, showing I was disease free, as expected.

Which meant, if I wanted to do this, I didn't have any reasons not to. Also, if I wanted to be able to pay for summer classes, I was out of time. I had to "woman up" making me equal parts nervous and excited.

"It smells good."

Mason's voice made my shoulders tense as I mixed the salad again. "Thanks, it's the chicken and leeks recipe. Not a big deal." It was. I mean, I'd had to make the marinade and let it soak overnight, but it was one of my favorite meals. Up until now, dinner had been whatever I could put in Mason's slow cooker and let it cook itself. I'd been surprised that Mason had a fully stocked kitchen. I'd found an Insta Pot in the pantry that I planned to try out once I got over my need to avoid him.

"How are your finals going?" he asked.

"Good. I have my last one in a few days. I don't think it's possible to study any more without melting my brain." I laughed, but it sounded fake.

"I was starting to wonder if you still lived here or maybe were just avoiding me." Mason's laugh was much more convincing than my own.

"What. *Pffft*. No. I'm not avoiding you. I've

been busy." I took a deep breath before blurting, "I might be a little nervous, which turned into really nervous because we never talk about it, so I've just being filling in the blanks and my imagination is insane. Do we kiss or not kiss? Who holds the camera? Will my butthole be on the internet forever? Because, believe me, enough people have seen it. Am I supposed to moan and thrash around? What do I do with my hands?"

My words died off when Mason walked around the counter to stand right in front of me, dipping his head so his eyes were level with mine.

"I don't want you to be nervous. You have total control of everything that happens. You can change your mind at any time. I'd love to kiss you, but we don't have to. The camera will be on a tripod. If you don't want something on camera, it won't be." The closeness of his body was making me hyper-aware of how easy it would be to lean in and put my mouth on his. The fact he could've laughed off my nerves but hadn't made something twist in my chest.

"I want you to react honestly, and I hope your hands will be on me." His fingertips grazed my chin with a ghost of a touch that made my breath catch. The look in his eyes was one of desire mixed with something I couldn't place, but in that moment, I knew he'd been thinking about us together just as much as I had.

Impatient, I leaned forward, needing to feel his lips on mine. Instead, with my eyes closed, I misjudged the distance, slamming my mouth against his in what was probably the world's most unsexy kiss. Heat flamed in my face as I pulled back licking my sore lip, but Mason's hands found my hips and pulled me up against his body as he tipped his mouth to meet mine.

This was the kiss I'd wanted. A kiss that I could feel *everywhere*.

Electricity shot up my body, tightening my nipples and making me lean against Mason's hard body. Maybe it had been too long since I'd felt someone else's touch. Or maybe it was the fact I'd never felt a touch from someone that lit up my body like his did.

I'd spent the last few weeks anticipating us in bed together. Fantasizing what it would be like creating an extended foreplay and a need that I hadn't been able to satisfy on my own.

"See? That's all you have to do. Just react however you feel. If you aren't enjoying yourself, that's my fault. Not yours." Mason spoke as he pulled back. His words sank slowly into my brain. My lips still tingled, and my body begged for his.

Holy shit, that was intense.

Mason already had me more turned on than anyone else ever had. From just a kiss.

Suddenly, I wasn't nervous anymore. I was very, very anxious to get started.

"So, is it ready?" Mason's voice sounded deeper than normal, and I could feel a pull low in my stomach.

"Yes." My own breathy answer was drowned out by the oven timer set for the food I'd completely forgotten about. Food was not what I was craving now.

"I'll grab plates. Do you want to eat at the table or island?" Mason had already turned to open the cabinet as I tried to get my breathing under control. Did I not affect him the way he affected me? Food was the last thing on my mind now even as I grabbed potholders to pull the baking dish out of the oven.

"Island is fine," I said when I realized he was waiting for my answer. "For someone who doesn't like to cook, you have a fully stocked kitchen." The need to fill the silence was overwhelming. I loved cooking. It was relaxing and fulfilling to make something that would nourish my body and make me feel good. But my body was still protesting the distance between our bodies and the amount of clothes we wore.

"I wasn't sure what you'd need to cook, so I tried to remember what you used at Chelsea's, and the saleslady offered a few tips."

"You bought all this stuff after I moved in?" I felt a little light-headed, letting myself lean back on the counter as I struggled to process my emotions. "Why?"

"Because you offered to cook, and you're good at it. I didn't want to miss out on meals because you didn't have whatever you needed."

His answer was straightforward, but it didn't ease the sudden tightness in my chest. I knew the prices of some of the things he'd purchased were more than I spent on books for a semester, like the very expensive standing mixer with all the attachments I'd wanted forever.

"Oh." I tried to figure out what this weird sensation was as Mason started making our plates

"Do you want a beer? Or wine? Wine goes better with chicken, right? I picked up a few bottles of the kind you drank before." Mason's voice sounded weird, and now I was glad my back was to him because I was taken off guard and was a little disappointed.

Did alcohol with dinner mean he didn't want to film tonight?

The fact that he had not only bought a kitchen full of small appliances and utensils for me, and then remembered the cheap wine I used to drink from a year ago, left me feeling confused. I told myself not to read too much into it. He did stand to make a lot more money if I participated; he was just trying to keep me comfortable so I wouldn't back out.

Mason and I got along. Neither of us had expressed any real interest.

"Wine." I answered when I realize he was still waiting for me to respond. "This will taste really good with a bottle of white wine."

I caught Mason's smile as he opened the beverage cooler to grab a bottle. It was cheap, but good, and it was the exact brand I'd drink if I had an extra ten bucks. Which, sadly, wasn't often.

"Is there anything you'd like me to make? Once finals are over, I'll have time until summer classes start." I hadn't planned on taking too many extra hours at the diner. I meant what I'd told Mel about enjoying myself more this year. Losing the scholarship had been hard, but it was a lesson that I could do everything right and work hard and things could still fall apart. I didn't want to look back and wish I'd had more fun.

"I really like that casserole you used to make. It tasted like tacos but looked like lasagna...?" Mason was making his plate while I opened the wine and poured it in the two glasses he'd set down.

"It's my mom's version of a Mexican lasagna. I'll add the ingredients to my shopping list." It was easy to make. It was one of the few things my mom would cook. Usually, she was tired after working and picking up extra hours whenever she could. I'd handled most of the cooking from the time I was old enough to cook without catching things on fire.

"And homemade pizza?" Mason asked looking hopeful.

I nodded, adding a chicken breast and leeks to my plate.

"Oh, and your homemade Alfredo, with the broccoli and chicken. And do you think you could make some of the breakfast muffin things we can freeze? Oh, and bread? I haven't had any homemade bread since I moved."

"I think I can manage all that." I laughed. I hadn't made homemade bread since Mason had moved out. It was time-consuming, and beside me, Mason was the only one who had ever eaten it. I didn't like making it unless I made the dough for several loaves. If I was going to make a mess, I figured I'd make it worth my while. When Mason and I had both lived with Chelsea and he'd learned I could make bread from scratch, he'd gone to the store and brought back all the ingredients, offering to pay me to bake him bread.

"Just make a list, and I'll get it," Mason said before taking a bite. He moaned an approval, closing his eyes and making me temporarily jealous of a piece of chicken.

"I'm barely paying any rent. Making you buy all the groceries seems unfair," I protest with a mouthful of food.

"You're doing the cooking and the cleanup. It's only fair."

"Fine. You help with the cleanup, and we will split the groceries." Because as much as I loved cooking, I hated cleaning up the mess I left behind.

"Deal. I really missed your cooking," Mason said quickly between bites.

"I've been cooking for you." I wanted to laugh, but I didn't when his look turned serious.

"It wasn't the same. The food was good—don't

get me wrong, everything you cook is good—but it was different." Mason chewed, looking thoughtful. "It's like I could tell you were avoiding me with what you cooked."

"I was busy." I made some weird noise that were supposed to mask my discomfort but just made me sound guilty. "How does pot roast and pulled pork make you think I was avoiding you?"

He raised an eyebrow. "For one, you never ate with me. Even if I waited around for you to come home. And second, while it was all good, you always made things you could toss in the crock pot in the morning and set it to shut off. This week felt like you were rushing the act of cooking when I know it's something you enjoy."

That sensation crept into my chest again. Mason's observations were all correct and making it hard for me to figure out a way to feel something other than suddenly guilty.

"I'll handle the cleanup if you want to chill out on the couch." Mason was already rising and clearing the dishes off the table, so I decided to refill my wine and enjoy the fact someone was willing to clean up after me.

"No chick flicks!" Mason called just as I'm settling on the couch.

I laughed as I scrolled through the movies, picking one that had me giggling as I pulled the throw blanket off the back of the couch.

"You're lucky I like this movie." He grinned pulling my feet into his lap, using his thumbs to rub the arches of my feet.

"Oh, my God, that feels good. And who doesn't like *Hot Shots*? Thank you for cleaning the kitchen. I know I waitressed for Rosa, but the diner is nonstop." That was an understatement. The family-owned Italian restaurant had business, but the diner was always slammed. Sure, the tips were good most of the time, but I ran my ass off.

What was even more relaxing was in this moment it was obvious Mason had been telling the truth. There was no pressure. No need to worry about what would or wouldn't be happening down the hall in that special room.

8

HIDE THE SALAMI

"Do you think you'll have time to make your cinnamon buns this week?" Mason was pushing the grocery cart that was already full as he looked longingly at an endcap display of cinnamon spice.

"If you help me with the bread and buns, then I can do them both together." Mentally, I checked to see if there would be enough room in the freezer for what we'd already bought and what Mason kept adding. If he didn't run every morning, I'd worry about his waistline. "We'll need to go back to the baking aisle."

After I'd made a quick breakfast this morning, Mason had suggested heading to the grocery store, both of us happily not talking about the fact I'd fallen asleep on the couch while Mason had rubbed my feet, but I'd woken up in my bed.

"I forgot to get salami. I love having it with your bread. Would you mind grabbing it while I hold our spot in line?" Mason asked as we headed to the check out.

"Sure." I made a U-turn and headed towards the back where the deli counters and lunchmeat were but stopped short when I realized there was actually more than one kind of salami. Chewing on my lip, I felt guilty because he'd remembered so much about the things I liked. I looked until I found a variety bundle and booked it back to the front of the store to see Mason already checked out.

"Can you get that, and I'll meet you at the car?" He gave me a wink and was gone before I fully realized I'd been played. Considering the mountain of food in his cart, I should've been happy to purchase the salami, but instead, irritation settled in my stomach. I wanted to make a scene about not getting a free pass, but my bank account wasn't exactly in the same ballpark as anyone else's in this store. The thirty dollars' worth of salami I was carrying was proof of that.

"I know I'm asking you to make a lot of food.

How about I treat you to lunch? Maybe we can order takeout while we make the dough…?" His tone indicated he was happy, and I didn't want to act like a petulant kid, but I was still irritated after slinging his dumb salami in the trunk and getting into the passenger side of his car.

"Are you ok?" Mason asked, but I ignored him, opting to scroll through my phone. I had a few texts. One from Mel, which I ignored since she was asking if I'd spent any naked time with my roommate. And one from my mom. It was a picture of matching onesies that said, "I have the best big sister." I responded with a promise to call soon. I needed to visit them.

"You sent me to find the salami so I wouldn't try paying for my half, didn't you?" Even though I'd told myself I wasn't going to say anything, the words were out of my mouth before Mason was even fully behind the wheel.

"I went a little overboard in there. If it bothers, you can pay me back." Mason shrugged like it was no big deal. His reasoning made me feel silly and my irritation subsided.

Deciding a change of subject was in order, I said, "How about Chinese? It's the perfect food when you plan on doing a lot of cooking because you're hungry after you eat it." My suggestion was only slightly based on the fact steamed dumplings were one of the few things I sucked at cooking.

"How's your mom doing?" Mason asked, catching me off guard, but I couldn't keep the smile off my face when I showed him the picture, she'd just sent me.

"It's weird knowing I'm going to have siblings and there's going to be such a big age difference between us. I do not envy my mom getting pregnant, but it's cool." I sighed. "I need to visit soon. They're both trying to work and save before the babies come, and I know if I don't go to them, they'll come here." I gave him a direct look. "And you could've just told me what you were doing instead of sending me off."

I might not have been mad anymore, but I wasn't completely over it.

"I didn't just send you off. I really did want salami."

I was having an oddly enough hard time maintaining my aggravation at him.

"Do you plan to visit your parents before summer classes start?"

"I was going to see how everything panned out."

"If you need money, Jules, all you have to do is ask."

And the irritation was back. But instead of making an ass out of myself, I nodded, keeping my mouth shut until we got back home.

"So, you made a good point." My mouth was full of salami and bread still warm from the oven. We'd spent the afternoon baking as we'd snacked on Chinese food. The kitchen smelled amazing.

"I knew you'd see it that way." Mason put his hand on my shoulder to reach over me to grab another slice of bread.

"I don't think I've ever made this much dough at once." We'd baked three loaves and had frozen the other nine. My fingers and forearms hurt from kneading it. Mason had tried to get me to use the stand mixer, but the bread was never the same. However, I had used the mixer for the cinnamon rolls.

The hand on my shoulder started massaging the tension from my body. Despite the mess in the kitchen, I started to relax, leaning back into him.

"I'll clean up," Mason whispered, his breath brushing my cheek like a soft caress that I feel everywhere in my body, making relaxing the last thing I want to do.

Turning in his arms, I went up on my toes just high enough to put my mouth on his. Just a light brush of my lips against lips.

"Or we could leave the mess for now." Tangling my fingers in his, I started to lead him towards my room. I could barely remember the last time I'd spent any naked time with a guy. And I'd never been as worked up as I was right now. I could feel the heat spreading throughout my body, the wetness between my legs.

I had thought that knowing Mason and I were going to end up in bed together at some point would've made our living arrangement awkward. Instead, it had kept my libido on a constant state of high alert. Wanting what I knew would happen, eventually, was worse than waiting for cake at a birthday party.

I was willing to work for what I wanted, but I always hated to wait for it.

Mason followed me easily, his fingers wrapping around mine. His free hand was on my waist, his fingers finding the bare skin just above my hip under my shirt.

"Are you sure?" Mason asked his voice so deep and husky it made my stomach clench—but then flip—when I realized he had pulled us to a stop outside his office door.

"Yes." My voice was breathless. I'd temporarily forgotten about the video. About needing the money and all my other problems. Being around Mason today had been nice, making me feel carefree and a little reckless. Those weren't feelings I was used to, and I wanted more of them.

Refusing to let any nerves creep in, I let him lead me into the office.

"It's just you and me, Jules." Mason turned to kiss me. It wasn't the light kiss I'd given him before. It was deep. Hot and messy with a promise of much more to come.

Remembering the videos, I'd been watching of him stripped away the very last reservation I had. Sliding my hands under his shirt, I felt the tight muscles of his abdomen as I pulled his shirt above his head.

"You are so sexy." My voice didn't sound like mine. The sultry tone was deep and sensual.

Mason's mouth was on mine again. Like two

people who couldn't get enough of one another, we were a flurry of hands caressing, rubbing, pulling, until the only material between us were my cotton panties.

My hand closed around Mason's shaft, making him let out a moan as a shudder racked his body. His hands found my breasts, and a thumb grazed my nipple. I tightened my grip.

"Condom or no?" Mason's voice in my ear sent a jolt of pure desire through me, making it impossible to focus on his words.

Somewhere in the back of my mind an alarm bell went off, and I wanted to silence it. Never had I been this reckless with sex. Sure, we'd both gotten tested and exchanged clean bills of health over my homemade chicken alfredo. This first time, I wanted there to be no barrier. Which startled me out of my lust-induced stupor.

"Condom." My heart was still pounding in my chest as I spoke the word. If it disappointed Mason, he didn't show it. He reached into the nightstand, and I could hear the crackle of the plastic wrapper. There is no awkward waiting for him to put the condom on that had happened to me before.

Pressing another kiss to my lips, Mason put a pink and black scalloped masquerade mask in place hiding the upper part of my face before putting on a matching on of his own.

"Don't think about the camera. It's just us. Just you and me." His lips dipped down my neck.

I had no idea what Mason was doing to me. This was supposed to be a paycheck. A blissful transaction between two willing parties for some toe-curling fun and financial security. The nerves I expected were nowhere to be found. In it's place lust and eagerness.

Raising up on my knees, I pushed on his shoulder until his back was flat against the mattress, and then I positioned myself above him and sank down.

Mason's hands on my hips acted as a guide, but he left me completely in control of the situation, staying still as my body adjusted to his size.

The pain of being stretched mixed with pleasure as I began to move my hips. Once I found the right rhythm, Mason's thumb dipped, rubbing slow circles against my clit that sent me to the edge with a moan on my lips. He increased the pressure against my nub, causing more glorious friction as my movements became more frantic until I was coming apart. The orgasm felt like nothing I'd ever had before. More earth-shattering than anything I'd experienced on my own or with another.

Shudders from my release made my thigh tense as Mason let me ride the high of my own pleasure before rolling me underneath him.

"You're so sexy when you come." His lips took mine and as he rocked his hips slowly, he caused aftershocks of pleasure to roll through my body. I wrapped my legs around his waist, angling my pelvis back and making us both shudder in pleasure.

"Fuck," Mason murmured. "Not going to last." His last word ended on a groan as he thrust harder, finding his own climax.

Mason was probably an amazing dancer.

Panting, I laid next to him, unsure of what happened now. Was a smack on the ass too blasé? Should we cuddle? Or should I get dressed, go back out into the kitchen, and clean the giant mess we'd left?

My body felt boneless as he got up to dispose of the condom.

From the kitchen, I heard the chiming of my phone; it was the ringtone I'd assigned for my parents. Jumping at the perfect excuse to escape, I grabbed Mason's discarded shirt and pulled it on as I rushed to make it to my phone.

I snatched it up just in time and began loading the dishwasher to have an excuse for being short of breath.

"Hey, honey." Mom's voice sounds even more tired.

"Hey, mom. How's it going?" Mason walks into the kitchen with a smile on his face, wearing only the jeans he'd had on before.

"Good. I had a few minutes before class starts and thought I'd call and see how your finals went."

"Good. I haven't gotten any grades back yet, but I feel confident I passed." Behind me, I could hear Mason filling up the sink to wash the dishes that weren't going to fit in the dishwasher. "I thought I'd come down for a night or two to see you and dad soon."

"That would be great, honey." I heard the smile in her voice. "Your father and I were just talking about driving up to see you, but if you come here, we can show you the progress we're making in the nursery. I saw a thing on Pinterest about using a twin bed as a daybed in a nursery since parents spend so much time in the babies' room. So, your bed is still there."

I felt a little twinge of something at the thought of my room no longer being mine. I hadn't planned to move back home after college, but now, the safety net was officially gone and it was a little more real—and scary.

9
LITTLE MAN IN A BOAT

I hadn't thought this through if the excited look on mom's face was any indication. When I'd told Mason I was going home this weekend to visit my parents, he'd offered to let me borrow his car. Which had snowballed into me inviting him to come along. Not that I didn't want to spend the weekend with Mason. I enjoyed his company. Once the initial shock wore off my mom's expression after I walked through the door with a guy, I realized she was going to read more into our relationship than it really was. Dad seemed less than thrilled to see that I'd brought a guy home, and even less so once I'd filled them in on the fact that Mason and I were living together.

"How have you been feeling?" I asked mom

trying to deflect any more questions about my roommate.

After a look over her shoulder to where dad and Mason were sitting on the couch, both pretending to watch TV while each watched the other, she gave me a tired smile.

"I'm so glad you're home, Jules. I've been trying to keep myself calm because I feel really unprepared for this." She rubbed her stomach. "I'm happy. We always wanted you to have siblings, always wanted a big family, but we kept waiting until we had more money, which never happened. What do you think the odds are that I'll get two more just like you?"

"You and dad are great parents. You've got this." I offered her a smile as I stirred the pot of spaghetti.

"You've always been a responsible person. I swear you were the oldest young person I've ever met. You made being a parent so easy, I feel like we spent so much time trying to get ahead that we worked too hard and missed too much."

"I don't think so." Sure, we hadn't taken the vacations my classmates had, but we'd taken trips to the park and zoo and had picnics in the backyard.

We'd done lots of things that had been free but had required a good imagination.

"Mason is nice."

"Mom, he really is just a friend."

"You keep saying that, but he looks at you like you've hung the moon. And I see you watch him, too. Are you two being safe? Because I think I should mention the only one hundred percent sure way to not get pregnant is anal."

"Mom!" Shocked and a little traumatized, my voice was loud enough to draw my dad's attention.

"Everything okay, honey?" Dad looked up from the couch, Mason following suit.

"I'm just warning our baby girl about the dangers of unplanned pregnancy."

My Dad's eyebrows rose. "Did you tell her the only safe sex is oral sex?"

My face was on fire. I let my gaze flick to Mason, who was as red-faced as mine felt.

My Dad's gaze swung to Mason. "Wait. Don't think about doing that to my daughter. Or anything, until you're married."

"Dad!" I looked at my feet, willing a hole open in the floor to swallow me. Anything to stop what was currently happening. "I'm sorry," I said, looking toward Mason, sure he was regretting his desire to be around a family only to find him laughing.

"I will only do what your daughter allows me to do, and I promise to only do it respectfully."

As Mason dried his eyes, my dad stared at him for a moment before turning back to my mom. "Do you think I should talk to him about the little man in the boat?"

I wasn't sure what bizarro world I'd walked into but my mom was flashing an evil grin as she gave him a thumbs up.

"Ok…well, son, you've got to sink the little man in the boat," Dad said turning his attention back to Mason.

"Do I even want to know what that is?" I murmured to my mom even though I was pretty sure I don't in fact want to know.

"It's your clitoris, dear. I know they probably didn't teach you in sex ed but there are two kinds of vaginal orgasms."

"Mom, please stop." I wasn't above begging.

"I'll stop if you tell me you're being responsible. Two forms of birth control because, sometimes, condoms break, plus, an antibiotic can make the pill ineffective—which I apparently forgot about." She laughed, gently tapping her stomach.

"I'm being responsible, and I'm fully aware of what it takes to have an orgasm. Happy? Now, please get dad to stop. Mason and I are friends and roommates. Nothing more." Unless I wanted to add coworkers of sorts.

"Dinner's ready!"

I'd already decided I wasn't going to ask Mason what my dad had been telling him. The tips of his ears are red, and I'd suffered enough humiliation for the night.

Grabbing the plates, I met Mason's gaze as uncertainty settled in. Barring any more sex pep talks from my parents and forgetting all the embarrassing moments from before this would be a good visit.

Mom talked about her plans for the nursery, and Dad seemed to really be enjoying his second job at the home improvement store. They discussed finding a bigger house since eventually this little two bedroom would feel a bit crowded with two kids running around it.

"Your parents are nice," Mason whispered to me as we washed the dishes. Mom snored lightly on the couch. Dad had left right after dinner for his shift.

"I think they're pretty great." Which I did. "I'm

sorry about earlier. I honestly didn't think they were going to jump to the conclusion that we were dating."

"It wasn't what I was expecting. They aren't the parents I expected."

"What did you expect?" I asked with a smile because no one ever expected the things that came out of my parents' mouths.

"I expected that they cared about you, but I don't think I knew both of your parents were teachers."

"They met in college." A year after they'd started dating, I came as a surprise. Mom had dropped out while dad had finished school, but after I was born she took classes at the community college to finish her degree. It wasn't the easiest of marriages, but anyone can see they loved each other.

Mason smiled. "If you could be anything without having to worry about money, what would you be?"

Pulling the plug on the soapy water, it only takes me a second to answer. "A chef. I could spend all day in a kitchen, even if it was crazy, and still be happy." Which was true.

"Then how did you decide to become a kinesiology major?" Mason leaned against the cabinet, crossing his feet at the ankles, and I can't help but let my gaze wander up his legs to his waist. Desire starts to pool low in my belly, the heat spreading upward until Mason lightly clears his throat.

"Oh. I was at a college fair, and a recruiter was talking about useless majors that kids waste a lot of money on and majors that have a good return on the investment. He kind of talked me into liking the versatility of my degree plan. I wanted something that gave me plenty of fallbacks and a decent salary after the degree."

"Chefs don't make good money?" Mason smiled, and I notice a dimple on the left side of his mouth I hadn't seen before.

"Reliable work with a livable wage is more my issue. Most small restaurants don't make it past year three. Sure, I could work in a cafeteria or chain restaurant, but most of the fun of cooking, for me, is being able to cook what I want how I want it."

"So, you would open a restaurant if you never had to worry about money?" Mason's words ignited a longing as I imagined running my own kitchen, but I tamped it down.

I lifted my chin. "What would you do if you didn't have to worry about money? What is your dream career?" I don't want to answer his question. The hall closet had dozens of vision boards my mom had created over the years for dreams that never got off the ground. I always thought it was heart-breaking.

I never wanted to have to give up my dreams, so I found it easier to never have any.

"Would it make me sound like a complete wuss to say I just want a family?"

Stunned, I stare at Mason. A husband and kids didn't fit into my five-year plan. Or even my ten-year plan. First, I wanted to graduate and get established in my career. Then I'd buy a home, something small and affordable, before I even thought about looking for a long-term relationship.

I realized my jaw had sagged just a bit at his admission, and I closed it. "Not if that's what you want. What about your degree?"

He shrugged. "That's the beauty of what I do. Most of it can be done freelance and from home. My mom worked from home selling jewelry. My dad was a real estate broker, and he worked from home as often as he could. So, it was nice having them there when I was little."

I could picture a young, curly-haired Mason laughing and running around with parents who both looked a little like him. A hollowness formed in my chest. It must have been so hard to lose that.

I often found myself missing movie nights with my parents and the living room campouts we would have when I was growing up. I couldn't imagine the amount of loneliness and longing Mason must have felt.

"I have an idea. Follow me." Taking Mason's hand, I put a finger to my lips and grabbed my purse before quietly slipping out the back door.

"Are you luring me outside to take advantage of me?" Mason whispered, and suddenly, that's all I could think about.

"Do you want me to take advantage?"

"I do." Mason smiled, pulling me close, his mouth nearly touching mine.

"What are we doing?" I asked because I couldn't make sense of what he made me feel. Was Mason flirting? My heart raced.

"I'm just following your lead, Jules." Mason's lips dipped down to kiss me before he stepped back while still holding my hand.

"When I was younger, my parents and I would have campouts in the living room. Movies, popcorn. Sometimes, there would be pizza. Dad would drag the mattress out of their bedroom, and we would all snuggle on it and fall asleep watching movies. It's one of my favorite memories growing up. We haven't done it since I left for college."

"So, we aren't sneaking out to the spot you took all your high school boyfriends to make out?" Mason grinned, gently leaning his body into mine.

Part of me wanted to snort. I'd had no interest in dating high school boys. Too much drama and work went with it. "I hate to disappoint you, but the only guy I dated was the guy who took me to my senior prom, and our relationship was a depressingly short-lived experience."

"Poor guy wasn't able to leave an impression?" Mason let his lips brush mine as he spoke. Then he pulled back when I tried to press my mouth to his, a dimpled grin still in place.

"Oh, he left one, but it wasn't good or one that left me wanting a repeat." Mason stiffened, pulling further back, his tense jaw making the air between us seemed charged until I realized how he must have taken my words. "I think he spent more time trying to figure out how to put the condom on than on the actual sex. He was incredibly nervous, and the entire moment was so awkward he couldn't look me in the face afterward."

"Poor guy." Mason chuckled, kissing me gently

and making my knees feel rubbery. "You have no idea how intimidating a sexy confident woman like you can be, Jules. Let's go get supplies for movie night before your mom wakes up."

Mason linked his fingers in mine and led me to his car as I tried to wrap my mind around what had just passed between us. Surely, if any of this meant something, Mason would say it, right?

He had been clear he didn't want his future family to know about his college profession.

10
IT'S A DUD

"Have you seen the milk duds?" Mason asked rummaging through the bags we'd spread out on the counter while trying not to wake up my mom.

A stop at my favorite pizza place, Redbox, and the little grocery store down the road, and we were set. Grabbing the yellow box, I gave them a shake before tossing them to Mason just as the microwave beeped, signaling the popcorn was ready.

"You shouldn't have let me sleep!" Mom yawned loudly as she walked into the kitchen. "I don't want to miss any of your visit." She paused, taking in the bags spread across the counter and tears filled her eyes. "Don't mind me, pregnancy hormones. It's been a long time since we've had a movie night." Mom pulled me in for a hug, squeezing me tightly.

"I put Mason in charge of candy while I got popcorn, and he went a little overboard," I teased, dumping the bag of candy on the table.

"Well, of course he did. He's a guy." Mom laughed wiping her eyes as she stepped back.

"The pizza will be cold by the time dad gets home, but it's better that way."

"What movies did you get?" Mom grabbed a candy bar from the pile as Mason handed her the small stack of movies we'd gotten.

"We haven't seen these yet. Good choices."

"I'm going to go set up the living room." I pulled the box out of the last bag. It had been Mason's idea to grab an air mattress. It would give him a place to sleep that wasn't the couch, and it would give me a place to sleep when I wanted to visit after my siblings were born.

"Need any help?" Mason asked as my mom sniffled again in the kitchen.

"I'll go grab some blankets and pillows while you get that unpacked." I nodded to the air mattress before going down the hall.

"This is really sweet." Mom met me in the hallway as I was pulling linens out of the closet.

"I'm sorry if your father and I took things a little too far earlier with the teasing. I know you said Mason is just a friend, but the only friend you've ever brought home is Mel. You're always so serious, but you seem relaxed around him. I like him if that helps." Mom took the worn quilt out of my hands.

Her words replayed in my head. Relaxed was the last thing I felt around Mason. When he was near, it was like every one of my nerves was at attention. Around him, I felt more alive and aware than I ever felt before. Sleeping together had only increased the intensity. Like a soft humming volume suddenly cranked to the max.

"I hope your parents won't mind I had to push the couch back a little to make it fit." Mason reaches to take the quilt from my arms.

"It looks good." Mom set a second blanket on the couch and handed Mason the pillows she'd tucked under her arms. "I know we just ate two hours, but I'm hungry and that pizza smells good."

"I'll make more popcorn. Mason do you want anything?" Asking was second nature. At home, he always asked me if he could get me anything, but once the words left my mouth, I saw mom watching me, and I knew this was more than a small thing.

I'd never been one to cater to others.

Part of my independence came from the belief that most people were the same.

Before Mason, I'd never wanted to take care of someone.

Sure, I'd helped my parents, but that was different. I grew up seeing my friends going on big vacation, having new phones, and trendy clothes. Things that for my parents were out of reach but I never felt like I had less. We didn't go to Hawaii for spring break but we had a luau in the backyard with an inflatable pool and fruit punch in tiki cups. I saw the way my dad's eyes lit up when mom came into a room. I have never doubted my parents love for each other or me.

I remembered when the guy I'd dated freshman year of college broke his leg skiing over winter break. I'd never offered him help. In fact, we'd broken up shortly afterward because he'd been too clingy, wanting me to baby him. I thought about Mason getting hurt and needing help. That thought left me feeling unsettled.

Seeing him smiling in my parents house brought up feelings completely new to me.

"I agree with your mom," he said. "The pizza smells great. I'm going to grab a couple of slices before the movie starts."

Mason's grabbing a couple of slices turned into bringing all the food into the living and filling the coffee table with the stash of snacks and pizza we'd bought. We were just finishing the beginning of the first movie when dad came home.

He grabbed a plateful of snacks and sat on the couch with mom while Mason and I lounged on the air mattress. Somewhere between dad getting home and the next movie I dozed off. When I woke up, Mason and I were alone on the air mattress, the flickering of the TV the only light in the room.

"Your parents went to bed not long after you fell asleep." My head was still on Mason's chest, so I could feel the words vibrating as he spoke.

"I'm sorry I fell asleep." I tried to move but Mason's arms tightened around me.

"I like cuddling with you."

"What are we doing?" I raised up just long enough to see his reaction. The TV threw shadows across his face, making him look thoughtful.

"Enjoying the greatness of the MCU…?" Mason smiled, but it didn't reach his eyes, making me think he feels just as lost as I do when it comes to us.

"That's not what I meant." Raising up, I leaned in to put my lips on his, making the air mattress shift and sending me off balance. I end up putting my nose in his eye which had us both laughing.

"I like spending time with you." His fingers gently brush my jaw. The small touch, paired with his words, making butterflies flutter in my stomach. "I didn't like worrying about you the other day, and when I saw you leave the library with Noah, I wanted to punch him," Mason confessed, his face so close his lips brushed my skin.

It took my breath away.

He leaned his forehead against mine. "I'm not used to feeling that way. I don't think I ever have before."

"I know the feeling," I whispered then held my breath because the moment seemed so intense. So real, it terrified me.

When his lips finally met mine, nothing else mattered. I was lost in the moment, my heart beating so rapidly I wondered if Mason could feel it. I'd run miles and had never felt a rush like this before.

Throwing my legs over Mason's hips, I moved so I was straddling his waist, our mouths never separating.

It wasn't until the light flicked on with an almost blinding intensity that I realized all of our movements were being broadcasted, loudly, by the air mattress.

Mom cleared her throat. "I'm just going to get some water, and maybe, just randomly throw this out to the room that there are condoms in the vanity. I'm not ready to be a mom again, and a grandma, in the same year."

Sliding off Mason's lap, I buried my face into the pillow. "I'm just going to die now," I mumbled and felt the bed around me shake with Mason's laughter. "Shut up!" I kicked out, yelping when my toes connected with something much harder. "You're not innocent here either." I moaned into the pillow.

"I disagree. I was just innocently watching my movie, having to read subtitles because you snore by the way, when you woke up and pounced on me."

Moving only enough to grab the pillow, I shoved it over Mason's face, barely noticing that the light was back out.

"Oh, my God that was embarrassing." Rolling onto my back, I stared up at the ceiling.

Mason shifted next to me. "Will you go on a date with me?"

"No." I wasn't completely serious, but my face

was still hot, and I felt like being difficult even though my heart was fluttering.

"I'm serious." Mason touched my arm, and the stubborn fit evaporated from me, taking with it most of the embarrassment.

"Okay."

Neither of us made it to the end of the movie, and when we woke up in the morning, we were tangled together.

11
VIRAL

"Do you plan to go back soon?" Mason's asked once we pulled onto the highway. I had to swallow back the lump in my throat. Oddly enough, I felt more emotional leaving after this visit than when I'd moved to college.

"I want to make sure I visit again before the babies come." Aside from the embarrassing moments during the first day, the rest of the visit had gone smoothly. Even though I was sure mom had said something because dad spent the rest of the visit side-eying Mason. "Did you have fun?"

"I did. It was nice. I hope I'm invited to the next visit." Mason offered me a smile, and I just nodded.

"Do you want to stop by the store before we go home?"

"Sure." Mason was looking at his phone as I pulled into the parking lot. After this trip, this is no denying the poor state of my own car. I told myself that looking online for a replacement couldn't hurt.

"I'm going to run in and grab a few things. Any requests?" I asked.

Mason was still staring at his phone when he shook his head.

Grabbing the few essentials and waiting in checkout took only ten minutes, but Mason was still staring at his phone when I returned.

"Are you okay?" He looked focused in a way I'd never seen before.

"I just need to check on something when we get back." Mason's tone felt like a stone in my stomach.

"What's going on? You're kind of freaking me out." I could already see the gates to Mason's condo.

"Nothing is wrong. I just need to get home and check on a few things." Mason couldn't get out of the car fast enough once I pulled into the garage.

"Okay," I said to myself after watching him practically run inside. I put the eggs and juice in the fridge before heading to Mason's office.

"It's viral," Mason muttered, and I had no idea what he was talking about. "Our video. It's already the top downloaded video." Mason seemed shocked.

"It's only been up a few days." Wasn't this a good thing?

"Allfans sent an email to our subscribers—" Mason's voice drifted off. "There are so many messages. Requests. Some of the offers are insane." He wasn't looking at me. He was staring at his phone, looking tense.

"I thought it was just a onetime thing." Not that I wouldn't enjoy more sex with Mason.

"They're willing to pay twenty thousand dollars for a live."

So, now I understand his reaction because my jaw dropped, too.

"*Each.* To each of us. Twenty thousand dollars. My subscriber list has doubled, Jules."

Twenty thousand dollars.

To have sex with an insanely hot guy, I thought I had feelings for.

It was like getting paid to eat ice cream. It was something you were going to do because you liked it, but getting paid for it just made it more awesome.

"So, we do it, right?" I asked, shrugging. Why wouldn't we? I'd be able to pay for my last year of school without taking any loans and have a little left over for books.

"You want to do it?" Mason was watching me closely.

"Don't you?"

"I guess so. Yeah." Mason pushed away from his desk and stood, rubbing the back of his head.

"What's wrong? Your face looks weird." His brow was drawn, and his lips pinched in a way that made him look constipated.

"Thanks, Jules." He laughed, but it didn't relax the tension in his body. "I thought we were going to date."

I opened my mouth then snapped it shut. "Is there a reason we can't do both? I mean, if you wanted to do the traditional relationship with me that ship has already sailed. Considering we're living together and have already slept together. What's some porn added in?" Once the words were out of my mouth, they felt heavy, making me want to take them back.

"I don't know if I like the idea of other guys watching you. Jacking off while looking at your body, wishing they were me." Mason's eyes darkened.

"I was actively trying to keep that image from

my brain, so thanks for ruining that," I said, my tone wry. "But since you said it, it's already happening, right?" I was going to need to mentally scrub this conversation from my brain. I needed to give myself a moment. "Do you think I like knowing people are watching you? Because I don't. I don't like the idea of anyone watching you. Or anyone that came before me." My breathing was deep, a feeling of possessiveness catching me off guard.

His gaze studied me. "And you still want to do more?"

"We've already done one video. It's out here. Apparently, a lot of people have seen it. It's an insane amount of money to do something we're going to do anyway." An odd sense of déjà vu hit me remembering it hadn't been long ago when our roles in this conversation had been reversed.

"Okay." Mason blew out a deep breath. "I'm not taking any more rent from you, but please, still cook for me."

Remembering our bags, I walked toward the garage. Mason followed me through the house.

"Here, let me." Mason took our bags out of the trunk.

Once inside, Mason walked toward the hall with our bags.

"Unless you have any requests," I called after him, "I thought we'd just have sandwiches for dinner. Although, I think I'm going to take a shower first."

He paused midstride, set down the bags and walked toward me. "Want some company?"

I nodded because I did.

Before I can take a step toward him, Mason wraps his arms around me, and suddenly, I'm airborne. I wrap my arms around his shoulders to make sure he doesn't lose his grip.

"My shower is bigger." Mason carried me through his bedroom into his ensuite.

"Are we okay?" I asked because it still felt weird between us. For a moment that seemed to stretch, Mason said nothing as he kept me in his arms.

"I don't know how to be in a relationship." Mason whispers.

His eyes bore into mine, the moment more intimate than anything I'd experienced before. His confession was so raw, I wanted to soothe his vulnerability.

"Me either. We can figure it out together."

He slid me down his body until my feet met the floor, and I could feel his hardness between us.

"You are so sexy." Mason tugged my shirt over

my head, planting light kisses along my collarbone. I was already pushing my jeans down my hips as he unclasped my bra. My body was eager for the pleasure that was about to come. Stepping out of my pants, I looked up to find Mason moving his own jeans down his hips, and I felt like a lioness ready to pounce.

This time, I took my time, letting myself drink in the sight of the man before me

Mason's body was a thing to worship. Lean, hard lines.

His hard length, begging to be touched, had me reaching out. Once my hand wrapped around him, he let out a moan.

"If you keep touching me, I'm not going to make it into the shower."

I could feel the tightness in his muscles as I rose up on my toes to playfully bite his neck.

Mason dipped, pulling himself from my grip to grab my thighs. Then he lifted me up his body, settling me against his. Wiggling my hips, I tried desperately to seek the connection that was so close.

Cool tile met my back as Mason leaned back, turning on the water. The sudden spray made me gasp as Mason shifted his hold, letting me slide onto his shaft.

"You feel so amazing." Mason's words sounded reverent as my brain was being overloaded by sensations—the water's warmth on my skin, such a change from the coolness at my back, Mason's body joined with mine, the sounds of approval coming from his mouth as our bodies rocked together.

Pleasure coiled in my body and I tightened my legs around his hips. Moaning, color exploded in my vision. Then I was panting and completely limp while Mason supported my body. Our heartbeats hammered together in time as his leaned his forehead against mine.

His lips gently kissed mine. As he slid out, I realized we'd forgotten to use a condom.

"What's wrong?" Mason's lips were still on mine as he speaks.

"I've never—" I pulled back just enough to be able to look into his eyes. "Without a condom, I've never done that before." I saw the shock widen his eyes and felt the sudden tension in his body before he spoke.

"I'm sorry. I—"

The sudden worry in his eyes pulled at something in my chest, making me want to soothe him. Unsure of what to say, I softly put my lips to his.

"It's okay." I kissed him. "I liked it. And we are protected."

"Let me do your hair…?" Mason was already reaching for the shampoo.

"Okay." But I kept my back to the tiles that were no longer cold against my skin.

"Are you going to turn around?" Mason asked with a dimpled smile, and I felt the heat rush to my cheeks.

"Of course." Turning, I stared at the swirls of color, trying not to feel overwhelmed by the fact that Mason and I went from roommates with monetary benefits to dating in the last twenty-four hours. Mason wanted kids. A wife, a family. I wanted a career. Was it too early to be thinking about this? We hadn't been on an actual date yet. The thought of something that serious settled like a weight in my stomach, ruining the post-sex bliss.

But the thought of him with someone else didn't make me feel any better.

The smell of mint hit my nose just before Mason's fingers started massaging my scalp, melting some of the tension from my shoulders, and I leaned into his fingers.

"I love the sounds you make when I touch you." I hadn't even realized I was making any noise until

Mason mentioned it, but then I became increasingly aware of the fact that I was in fact moaning as he washed my hair.

"Seriously, Jules," he said, his voice husky, "you drive me crazy."

My breath caught because I knew exactly what he meant. Even if I wasn't sure why.

"When do we need to make our next post?" I wanted to shove the words back down my throat because they changed the mood of the shower. Something was gone once I'd mentioned it, even though Mason started rinsing my hair.

"We can do it whenever you want." Mason's voice was hollow, making me wish all over again that I hadn't brought it up.

12
TEABAG

"I can't believe you took him home to meet your parents before even telling me you're dating!" Mel leaned across the small table to shove my shoulder.

"Technically, we didn't start dating until *after*. He offered me his car, and I panicked and asked if he wanted to come with me. One thing led to another..." Grabbing some napkins, I dabbed the tea that had spilled over the rim of my cup.

"So, you don't want to be in a relationship?" Mel's voice got serious, drawing the attention of the people around us.

"Can we not tell everyone in here my business please?" I groaned, regretting that I hadn't waited for us to get back to her place before saying anything.

"Are you dating him just to have a place to stay? Because if you're that hard up, you can crash with me." My best friend was territorial about her own space. Growing up the oldest of five, she'd complained to me before that she'd hated sharing everything. Her offer was a huge concession. One I would never take her up on.

"No." I bit my lip, wanting to tell her everything. "It's just not part of my plan, you know? The sex is phenomenal. Mason is thoughtful and sweet. Almost annoyingly so, but…" I let my words trail off. I couldn't tell her he'd been weird since our video went viral without telling her we'd made a video in the first place.

"But? Does he have a thing? Like a weird kink? I slept with this guy once who needed to finish in my armpit. You know how I always say I will try anything once? That was one I didn't even see coming." She snorted at her own bad pun as I just stared at her. "So, what's his weird kink? If it's a deal breaker, don't feel guilty. Just enjoy the fun you had."

"First, I love you for how supportive and open-minded you are. Second, it's not a weird kink. Sexually, I have zero complaints. I get your pep talk from the night at bar now. Mason knows how to work his hips and hands." And mouth because before I'd left he'd given me an incredible orgasm as I'd lain spread across the kitchen island.

It had been a week since we'd decided to date, and we'd fucked on nearly every surface of his house. But we hadn't been back inside the office.

"I knew you were holding out on me when you started getting waxed." Mel's attention strayed to a barista behind the counter, the same one who'd paid for her drink. "So, it's not a kink. What's wrong?"

"I think I'm just not used to sticking to my plan," I lied, taking a big drink of tea and knowing I'd earned the burned tongue.

"I know exactly what you need." Mel smirked. "What we both need. A night out, and your new boyfriend can be the DD."

"I don't know." It sounded like a terrible idea. I wasn't looking for another hangover, but dancing would be fun.

"Come on, it'll be fun. There's going to be this party off campus. You said you were going to start having fun, and once classes start again, that's going to be harder." She clasped her hands together, pretending to beg.

I rolled my eyes before giving her a smile.

"Okay. I'm in."

"Yes!" Mel started clapping, ignoring the looks from everyone around us. "Now, text your boyfriend and tell him to pick us up from my place at nine. We have three hours to get ready and pre-game. Better to drink the quality liquor here. It makes the drivel of cheap drinks easier to swallow."

That was my best friend, a woman of expensive tastes.

By the time my phone chimed a text from Mason letting us know he was on his way, Mel had had me curled, contoured, highlighted, and wearing a bodycon dress with nude pumps. Determined not to experience another hangover, I kept my pregaming to a minimum even as butterflies swirled in my stomach.

This would be the first time Mason and I had been out as a couple—unless I counted trips to the grocery store. Which I didn't. We'd had massive amounts of sex in the last week. We'd eaten meals together. Watched movies snuggled on the couch, which ended in a foot rub for me or in heavy petting that led to orgasms.

But tonight, we would be going out, and I had

no idea how to act.

"You really like him, don't you?" Mel asked, watching me pace by the front door.

"Yes. Maybe. I don't know. I feel overdressed."

"You look hot, babe."

"Not half as hot as you, babe." I tossed her a wink.

"Just so you know, I consider that dress a gift to you, so don't try to return it after the hot sex you have in it tonight. That way, you don't worry about staining it, and toss it if he tears it. We'll enjoy a good time, and you can thank me by telling me all the details."

The doorbell saved me from having to reply. Taking a deep breath, I held it as I opened the door and waited for Mason's reaction.

Which was a stunned look.

"Let's get this party started!" Mel squeezed passed me, pulling me out the door. "Looking good, Mason," she said, locking her door. She wasn't wrong. In dark wash jeans and a navy shirt, Mason looked delicious.

"You look beautiful." Stepping around Mel, Mason pulled me against his chest, rubbing his fingers against the base of my skull as his lips devour mine. "I missed you today."

"Uh…" I sputtered, my mind blanking as Mason led us to his car.

"Smooth, Jules." Mel snorted. "I'm calling shotgun this time because I really don't want to watch my bestie give out handies on the way to the party." Ever the classy one, Mel mimed jacking off before slapping my ass as I climbed into the back seat.

It wasn't until we walked into the smaller two-story house, and I see Noah that I realize the party was being hosted by the baseball team in celebration of finals being over. The music was loud, the beer cheap, and the hard liquor even cheaper. It was perfect. Mel and I danced until my feet hurt and my hair felt heavy with sweat. Mason went to get us water while we waited on the back deck in night air that was only slightly cooler than inside the packed house.

"Jules, do you have a minute?" Noah's voice pulled my attention from Mel's description of what she'd like to do to the varsity short stop.

"Yeah."

"I'm going to head in and see if Calvin is still on the dance floor." Mel gave me a wink before strutting back inside.

"Your teammate might be in trouble." I laughed watching my best friend sway her hips.

"Anyone that Mel's choosing to give her attention to is a lucky man." Noah chuckled. "You came here with Mason. Are you two a thing now?"

"Yeah. I guess we're a thing." God that sounded lame to me.

"You guess?" Noah grinned.

"We are. It's just new and unexpected. I'm getting used to it." I forced a smile.

"You don't sound very excited."

"How is your summer going?" I asked to change the subject. I was happy to be with Mason even if he confused me. It felt like we were a couple, yet we'd never discussed it. Beyond Mason wanting to keep his college job a secret from anyone he dated in the future. Did that mean we would only be what we were now? It hadn't bothered me before. Now it did.

"Training has been rough. I'm taking an extra class this summer. A lot of the guys aren't taking any."

"That's a good idea." I said knowing I hadn't been paying attention. Clearing my throat, I forced my focus back to Noah.

"That's why I wanted to talk to you. I barely passed my A and P exam. It sunk my GPA. The professor is letting me submit a paper to help boost my grade. Coach will bench me if I don't ace this project." Noah shrugged. "I was hoping you might look it over before I turn it in. I had to give an in-depth explanation of the endocrine system then do a case study mockup."

"Want to meet at the library tomorrow? I work until noon, but I can head to campus after that."

"Thank you. I'll owe you huge." Noah leaned in a little closer. "So, care to tell me why you didn't sound so enthusiastic about your new relationship status? Mason is a really good guy. Catching your eye makes him lucky, too. If there's something bothering you, talk to him."

"It's just unexpected. I've never been in a serious relationship before, and things with Mason seem serious. I mean, we're living together, but it started as roommates. We lived together at Chelsea's and always got along. I guess I just have no idea what I'm doing, and I don't want to mess things up. Or make my life complicated. I never really planned on getting serious with anyone until after I'd settled into a career."

Talking about my personal life with someone I didn't know well wasn't something I'd usually did.

But then again, up until a month ago, I'd never have thought I would be a porn star, so I guessed things had a way of changing.

"So, you're serious about him then?" Noah asked and I could see the flicker of disappointment in his eyes.

"I don't know. Sometimes, it feels too serious for how new it is." I blew out a deep breath and looked up.

"Do you care about him?" Noah asked.

"Yes."

"Does he care about you?"

"I guess…?" Thinking about Mason and all the little things. The trip to my parents. All the appliances in his kitchen. "Yes." The revelation made my stomach sink. Was he doing all that for me or because I was making him a lot of money? Mason wouldn't use me like that. Would he?

What if he'd suggested dating as a way to keep making videos? After all, if I started dating someone else, it wasn't like I would keep sleeping with Mason.

"Relationships are complicated," Noah said. "I've only dated one girl seriously. She was my high school sweetheart, and we made all these plans. Things seemed simple and great, but once we got to college, she decided to date other guys without telling me about it."

My mouth dropped open.

"I drove up to her school to surprise her on our anniversary. Coach was pissed I'd skipped a practice, but I had this whole plan in my head. I'd bought a ring. I was going to surprise her with flowers and propose. Only she surprised me because I caught her bringing a date home to her apartment."

"That twatwaffle!" I blurted out, making Noah laugh.

"It sucked, but I got over it. The best advice I can give you is to be honest with each other. If you can't talk to him about whatever is on your mind, then it's probably not going to work out in the long run. If that's what you're looking for…" Noah leaned against the deck railing.

"I don't know what I'm looking for. Is that bad?" Mason wanted to keep how he'd made his money a secret from his future family. That would be impossible with me. Feeling like my heart was sinking, I took another drink.

Noah tossed his head back and laughed. "You're still in college, Jules. I don't think anyone is going to blame you for not having every moment of your life mapped out."

I wrinkled my nose. "You aren't the first person to tell me that."

"Talk to Mason. If you want different things, it's better to know sooner rather than later."

"Thank you." Caught up in my emotions, I lean in and give Noah a hug that he returns with a chuckle.

"Just so you know, your boyfriend is heading this way, and he's giving me a death glare," Noah whispered before moving away from me. "Hey, man. She's all yours. Jules, I'll catch you later."

"Mel said she was getting a ride home." Mason handed me a bottle of water and took Noah's spot next to me. "Are you having a good time?"

"It got better now." I'd had fun dancing. I'd gotten a chance to prove Mel's hypothesis because Mason was in fact a great dancer.

"Are you ready to go, or do you want to stay longer?"

Closing the distance, I made my preference clear by putting my lips on his. I knew we had things to discuss. But for once, I didn't want to overthink things. I wanted to seize the moment and enjoy the present without the pressure of thinking about the future.

I sent Mel a text, letting her know we were heading out but reminding her to message me when she got home. Mason led me toward his car, his hand on the small of my back. The car ride home was spent in an easy silence, charged with the feel of his hand on my thigh. His thumb rubbed circles against my inner thigh. I owed Mel huge for convincing me to wear a dress. They were wonderfully accessible.

By the time he pulled his car into the garage, I felt like I would explode if his hand didn't move the few inches over to my core.

As if he'd read my mind, his fingers brushed against the barrier of my underwear, pushing them aside. Once the car was off, he twisted in his seat. His mouth devoured mine as his finger stroked my clit.

"Don't stop, Mason." I panted because I was embarrassingly close to having an orgasm, and if he stopped now, I was pretty sure I'd die, or my vagina would go berserk and cause some serious damage to something. "Please," I begged.

"Because you said please." He slipped a finger inside as his thumb continued rubbing circles against my clit until it was all too much. This time, I was aware of all my moans as I come around his fingers, but I'm too satisfied to care.

When I opened my eyes, I found Mason looking smugly at me, and I could only smile. I felt completely boneless.

"How do you do that?" I whispered, breathless. "How do you manage to always know exactly what's going to blow my mind?" Because no other guy I'd ever done anything with had been able to get me as riled up as Mason. He never disappointed. I was pretty sure this could count as my cardio for the week if the pounding of my heart was any indication.

"I could say the same thing about you." Mason reached out to push my hair behind my ear, and suddenly, I don't feel so satiated. Moving in the confines of his car, I crossed the center console to straddle his lap.

His lips were on mine as I work on getting his pants down, leaning back to give myself better access. The sudden blaring noise of a horn made me jump, cramming my head into the visor. Pain jolts the back of my head and I curse, making Mason laugh, which made me laugh. The jiggle of my breasts caught Mason's interest, and like a light switch, the moment was back. His teeth grazed a nipple through my dress as I ground against him.

That's when I realized that the door to the garage was open, and a middle-aged man was watching with wide eyes what I could only imagine was a wildly rocking car.

"Oh my God!" I squealed and jerked down, wondering if the windows were tinted enough to keep him from seeing everything. Reaching my hand backward over my shoulder, I felt around for the garage door opener attached to the visor. I must have hit it when I'd slammed my head against it.

"Who saw us?" Mason was trying to hold back his laughter.

"Middle-aged guy, bald, with a fanny pack." I was cursing the well-lit street right now.

"Mr. Rempkin." Now, Mason was flat out laughing.

"It's not funny." I smacked him but keep my chest pressed against his.

"It kind of is, given our employment."

Oh, God. It was. I laughed at myself because the irony of the situation wasn't lost on me.

"Maybe I should check and see if we gave the poor guy a heart attack."

Mason chuckled lightly kissing my neck.

13

DID YOU TRY BLOWING ON IT?

"Hey, Jules." Noah called behind me, sounding breathless. "I was worried I was going to keep you waiting. I overslept and had to make up a training session." Panting, he held up a bag. "I didn't know if you'd be hungry, but I thought the least I could do is grab one for you."

I was starving. I could still smell the grease from the diner, and I tried to avoid fried food, which meant I was always starving after work.

"Noah, you are a life saver." I held open the door to the library.

"Turkey on wheat is the least I could do."

"Fair enough. Let's get a study room, and I can read over your paper while we eat."

"Uh, the endocrine system always trips me up."

Once inside our room, Noah pulled out two sandwiches wrapped in wax paper out before sliding a small stack of papers in front of me.

"The endocrine system is responsible for producing hormones that regulate things like metabolism, reproduction, growth and development, muscle and tissue development, mood and sleep." I took a giant bite when I heard my phone chime a new message. Not wanting to linger on campus any longer than necessary I kept reading Noah's project.

"That's a lot. It always trips me up." Noah sounded nervous.

"It's not so bad. This is good, so far." I nod to the paper before taking another bite.

"I like the house most of us players live in, but sometimes, it gets a little noisy. I've thought about trying to get a place of my own, but I think I'd get lonely. I grew up with three older sisters, so I'm used to being around people. The noise isn't always great for studying."

"I'm an only child, so I don't mind quiet. Or at least I was an only child." It was still a little unbelievable that I was going to be a big sister. "I'd probably be a raging bitch if I had to keep living in campus housing. There are too many people in the dorms. Too much noise for me."

"That has to be weird, being in college and getting a new sibling."

"It is. I mean, it's not like I have to worry about sharing my toys or anything." I laughed. "I'm excited, I guess, but it is weird. I'm going to be twenty-four years older than my little brothers. I'll be my parents' age when they're graduating high school." And I didn't envy them for that.

"I'm the baby of the family. I couldn't imagine my parents having more kids now. I'm pretty sure my mom would want to kill my dad." Noah laughed. "Do you think using Graves' disease as the basis for the case study was a good idea?"

"I'm not going to fact check you. This looks good. I think it's a solid project, especially on short notice." I pushed his project back to him then wadded up the empty wax paper and tossed it in the trash can.

"What happened to your arm?" he asked.

"I caught a hot plate to the wrist. It doesn't hurt so bad now. I've got some salve I can put on it when I get home."

"On that note, I should probably let you get back home. Thank you."

"Jules?" Mason paced the kitchen. "You weren't answering your phone."

"My battery died." I kept walking towards my room because I was overdue for a shower.

"I thought you only worked until noon." Mason matched my stride.

"I did, but Noah needed help studying."

"Noah is smart. Like, he makes the dean list smart." Mason touched my elbow, making me stop just before I reached the door to my room.

"Are you jealous?" I'd never dated anyone long enough to get to a jealous stage.

"Should I be? I see the way he looks at you, Jules." Mason let my arm go.

"Of course, you should be," I quipped. "I'm a catch and being jealous means you care. But you should trust me enough to know there isn't anything to be jealous of, even if it does make me feel desirable."

"I was worried that something had happened." Mason's level of concern had already exceeded what I was used to from my parents. Which, as much as I loved them, I was convinced they were relieved by how independent I'd always been, giving them less to worry about.

I wondered if they would be so lucky this time.

"My phone died," I repeated. It seemed lamed, but it seemed even lamer to admit I didn't think he'd would care that much. "I'm sorry I missed lunch. I didn't mean to be out so late."

"It's fine. I just got worried when you weren't texting me back. I didn't know if something had happened. Or maybe that your car had broken down. I've gotten used to you being home I guess."

It was the vulnerable tone of his voice that made my stomach swirl. "I didn't mean to make you worry." Wanting to comfort him, I reached out to tangle my fingers in his.

"I ordered Chinese for lunch."

"Sounds great. I'm going to jump in the shower really quick. Give me ten minutes, and I'll meet you in the living room. You can pick the movie." I headed to my room, stopping long enough to plug my phone in. Not wanting to keep him waiting again, I rushed through the shower and pulled on a pair of yoga pants and a tank top. When I entered the living room, I found Mason sitting on the couch watching me.

"I'm sorry about earlier. When I couldn't get a

hold of you, I panicked, thinking something happened."

"I'm not used to having anyone care when I'm home," I whispered.

"I always cared, Jules. I like spending time with you. I know this will sound a little weird, but cooking with you reminds me of when I was kid, helping my grandma in the kitchen. She loved to cook, and I loved sharing those times with her."

I took a seat next to Mason on the couch, and he spread the take out on the coffee table, but I couldn't keep my eyes off him. This felt like something big had passed between us.

"She raised me after my parents died when I was in grade school. My grandpa died before I was born, so it was just us. She died just before I left for college."

I tried to think of what it would be like to be alone. Without any family. I remembered all the times Mason had lingered around in the kitchen when we'd lived at Chelsea's. I'd never heard him talk about family. He'd never gone home for Christmas. Never had I realized it was because he didn't have a family to go home to. Suddenly, I felt homesick for the first time in a long time. Not going home wasn't because I didn't love my family or had a bad relationship with them. It was the result of growing up in a house with two parents who'd worked to keep our bills paid. I didn't have the luxury of being a lazy spoiled teen. When I'd wanted a car, I'd worked until I'd saved enough to buy my trusty rusty. My parents had always paid for everything I'd needed, but most of what I'd wanted I'd had to get for myself.

"What was your favorite thing to cook with her?" I leaned back, letting my body settle next to his.

"She used to make noodles from scratch. We ate them a lot because they were cheap. Sometimes, she'd cook them with chicken or beef. By the time she took me in, she'd already had a stroke, so she wasn't very mobile and her arthritis didn't help. I remember the noodles the most because we made them every week."

"I'm sorry you lost her." I meant it. I'd never lost anyone in my life, but it was in his voice how much he missed her.

I was glad I'd invited Mason to visit my parents and vowed to do it more often. Both to spend more time with my family and for Mason's sake.

We spent the night cuddling on the couch. It wasn't the first night we'd spent together, but it was the first time I'd woken up still cuddled next to him.

I woke up before Mason and watched him sleep. Which was something I'd never understood before, but now my heart fluttered. It had only been weeks since the day that had turned my world upside down, threatening the path I'd thought I wanted.

I'd spent the first three years of college constantly pushing myself to work harder for my future. If it hadn't been for Mel, I don't doubt I'd have had any fun.

"Are you watching me sleep?" Mason asked, his eyes still closed.

"Busted," I confessed then decided to go further. "Not a restaurant," I whispered.

"What?" Mason opened his eyes.

"Before, you asked if I wanted to open a restaurant. I don't. But I have always wanted to work in my own kitchen to cater or offer take-out meals that are ordered in advance. I love cooking, and nutrition plays such an important part in our health." I'd never said it aloud before. Never let it grow big enough to be more than a passing thought.

"You should do it." Mason sat up, pulling me with him. "You're an amazing chef."

I didn't say anything. I didn't want to spoil the moment, giving him all the reasons for why I knew it would never happen. Not when he made me feel like it could. That it was at least trying. It felt wild and dangerous.

"I can think of something else I would rather do." Grinning, I stood, extending my hand. Mason took it without hesitation as I led him to the office.

My reservations about the videos were gone in the face of the emotions Mason brought to the surface.

"You're sure?" Mason asked as we cross the threshold.

I didn't trust my voice, so I nodded.

This wasn't like the first video when I'd been so desperate for Mason that I'd gotten lost in the moment. I was fully aware as he grabbed his camera and set up the tripod. This time didn't feel like the times we'd been together, without the camera, either.

14
THAT'S GOING TO LEAVE A MARK

"You are practically glowing," Mel said as she flopped on my bed. "This whole enjoying life thing suits you."

"Shut up," I grumbled.

"Uh, oh. Is there trouble in paradise?" Mel sat up.

"No." Though Mason had been distant. It had been days since our last video. I had experienced a shellshocked moment when I'd checked my bank balance after Mason had said the royalties had been paid out. Since then, he claimed he had an extra coding project, and except for meals, I barely saw him.

"I think you and my mom were right." I used to think the worst possible future would be one that left me in crippling debt. Now that I was letting go, I had a new perspective. "Would you think I was crazy if I said I was having doubts about my major?"

"For you? I might be worried. For any other college student? I think we all change majors and career paths." Mel laughed until she realized I wasn't joking. "Really?"

"You're right. It's crazy."

"Good dick can scramble your brain."

"Speaking of... You haven't overshared about your night with the short stop." I grinned.

She grimaced. "If I'd known the name was more than just a position on the field, I would've made sure to see him dance first."

"Are you traveling this summer?" I asked as I heard Mason's voice in the living room.

"I leave at the end of the month."

"Do you know where you're going?"

"Mykonos. I'm so excited to go to Greece." Mel gave me a weird look as another voice joins Mason's and got louder in the hall outside my bedroom.

"Hey, Jules." Noah leaned into my partially open door. "Mel." Noah looked around my room. "I am such a bad friend. You know, I didn't even bother to ask you how you liked your job at the diner the other day."

"It's fine. The hours are flexible, and the tips are good." I made more there working fewer hours, so I didn't even mind if I always left smelling like greasy food.

"Good. Good." Noah was still looking around my room in a way that had Mel and I exchanging looks.

"How did your project go?" I asked.

"Oh, good. It was good. I'll let you get back. I need to talk with Mason some."

"What was that?" Mel whispered as Noah disappeared.

"Absolutely no idea."

"You should come with me. To Greece."

"I can't. I couldn't get time off work, and I want to spend more time visiting my parents before classes start again."

"How is your mom doing?"

"Good. She was asking if you're going to come visit soon." Which reminded me that I'd never told her about Mason joining me for my last visit. "I feel like I haven't seen you much lately."

Mel laughed. "We see each other as much as always. The only difference is, now, you have something more going on than just work and school."

I opened my mouth to respond, but a thud sounded, followed by a shout.

I was off the bed and down the hall with Mel at my back, following the sounds to find Mason and Noah fighting in the living room. The coffee table was upended, and both men looked disheveled and bleeding.

"What's going on?" No one acknowledged my question, so I raised my voice to tell them to stop.

"Are you sleeping with him?" Mason asked, punching Noah one more time before shoving him away.

"What? No. Why would you even say that?"

Mason's eyebrows lowered. "He's been watching you."

"Mason, do you have a concussion? You aren't making any sense."

"He knows about the freckle on your breast."

My jaw dropped.

"Jules had a nip slip out at the bar the night we all came back here." Mel stepped up. "Do you plan on fighting everyone there who saw her breast?"

Mason and Noah stared at each other. Both were breathing heavy, and I swore the world felt like it tilted, like one wrong move was going to topple everything. Noah's gaze met mine.

"Don't look at her." Mason growled. I didn't even know it was possible for his voice to sound that lethal.

"You're taking the caveman routine a little too far," Mel said, as I still couldn't find my voice.

Then it hit me. No one was supposed to know.

"They don't show my face," I finally spoke, whispering, and it drew the attention of everyone to me.

"What are you talking about, babe?" Mel whispered to me. She must have noted my expression. My face felt as though all the blood had drained away.

"The freckle could've been anyone." Noah wiped blood from his mouth. "I thought… I wanted to think it was you. But it was the burn…" He nodded to my wrist. "I saw it when you were helping me with my paper. Then I saw it in the video."

"What video?" Mel asked.

"Juliet is making videos for Allfans." Noah looked at me, and his eyes were full of disappointment. "I didn't think you were the type."

"I told you not to look at her." Mason lunged at him, and the two begin fighting again.

"Stop!" Mel and I both yelled together.

With my heart in my throat, I pushed my way between them. "Noah, you need to go." I pushed against his chest lightly but couldn't meet his gaze. I was too afraid I'd see more disappointment there.

"I'm going to walk him out—if you will be okay?" Mel asked, looking between me and Mason. I nodded, keeping my eyes lowered.

"He was watching you," Mason repeated.

"We knew that was going to happen."

"Not someone we knew. Not someone that knew you. Someone who was already trying to get into your pants." Mason turned his anger on me. "Is that where you were the other day? Did you fuck him? Is that why he came here to rub it in? It's a shame you didn't film it. It would've paid off your parents' house."

I jerked back. His words had hit harder than a physical blow, making my eyes sting. Turning my back on him, I went to my room and grabbed Mel's bag and my own.

"Where are you going?" Mason followed me, and I forced myself to swallow the knot in my throat.

"Anywhere that is away from you. You are so out of line. I helped him with an extra credit project. I didn't lie about that. I'm not fucking anything but stupid, and as of five minutes ago, you. Which apparently was a bad financial decision. Thank you for enlightening me about my foolishness." I dodged his hand as he reached out. "You do not get to touch me."

"Jules…" Mason dropped his hand then ran his fingers through his hair. "I didn't mean it."

"Which part? The part where you assume because we've been sleeping together you get to act like a jealous asshole? Or that the fact that we've both been making money from us fucking, but somehow I'm the whore now?" I was yelling as Mel came back inside. She took my hand with a nod and led me toward the front door.

"Jules, wait. I'm sorry. I know I have no right—"

"Exactly, you have no right," I tossed over my shoulder without looking back.

"Please, don't go."

I walked to the driveway, still not looking back. "I don't want to be here. Neither of us is in the state of mind to talk anything out."

"I'm—"

"I don't want to hear it, and if you keep talking

right now, I probably won't ever want to hear it," I said, slamming Mel's car door.

"Do you want to talk about it?" Mel asked as we pulled away.

I tried and failed to not watch Mason in the sideview mirror. The wrecked look on his face made my eyes sting with unshed tears.

I nodded.

"So, you guys…" Mel cleared her throat. "Allfans, huh? That explains how he can afford his place and that car."

I sniffed. "Can I stay with you for a few days?"

"You don't even have to ask."

With that, I burst into tears.

15
BARE IT ALL

"I've let you mope for an entire day. Now, it's my duty to end the pity party. Talk to me." Mel bounced on her bed again.

I groaned, remembering the last time I'd been in her bed with a hangover. If only I had a time machine.

"Okay, so if you aren't going to talk, I will. I had Noah send me the link to your account. First, damn girl, its hot. I wish I would've known Mason would be that good in bed. I would've done more than kiss him freshman year." Mel fanned herself dramatically.

I sat up, seeing red.

"Is there anyone on campus you haven't fooled around with?" Jealousy burned through my body even as I regretted my words. Mel's nostrils flared, pain showing in her eyes for a brief second become she schooled her features.

"It's a pretty big campus, despite my best efforts, I'm sure I've missed a few. What bothers you more —that I'm not so rigid that I can enjoy my life? Or are you just jealous I'm not afraid to own who I am and what I want?" Mel raised her eyebrow.

Her words had bite, and I clenched my jaw to keep myself from saying anything else.

"You are the most repressed person I have ever met, Juliet. I used to think you were focused and driven. Not afraid to follow your passion. But honestly, you are just so full of bullshit. You are scared to try anything that might make you step out of your comfort zone."

"I'm pretty sure posting a video of me having sex with someone was a big step out of my comfort zone!" I shot back.

Mel rolled her eyes. "It's funny that you think that's what I'm talking about, without even recognizing how wrong you are. You didn't show your face. No one knows it's you, and Noah figuring it out was a fluke. It's the fact you fell for Mason and are too chicken shit to do anything about it. You keep saying there are no feelings there, but you two do everything a couple does, all the while worried someone might actually think you're human because you make a mistake or get scared by what you're feeling."

I lifted my chin. "Mason was clear that what we do is business. He has a plan for having a family that doesn't involve anyone knowing about any of it." God, my reasoning sounded weak to my own ears.

"Odd you found the one guy on campus that has the same goals and motivations as you, and yet you won't tell him how you feel."

"It's not like that between us." But it was. I was full of shit, and like a true friend, Mel was calling me on it.

"Then why did he try to beat the shit out of Noah? You do realize that if Noah got hurt and can't play, he won't get drafted, right? That his dream will gone because you couldn't put on your big girl panties and be honest with the people around you."

I sucked in a big breath.

"Yes, Jules, other people have problems, too. Not just you."

"I know other people have problems."

"Or how about the fact that Noah was acting

weird because, once he figured out it was you, he had no idea Mason knew and went to him, trying to warn him that his girlfriend was cheating."

Fuck me. She was right. I had nothing to say. I was a giant asshole as far as Noah was concerned. His look of disappointment made a lot more sense now.

I sighed. "I don't deserve it, but can I borrow your car?"

"I don't know. I might have screwed the entire junior class in the backseat." Mel tossed my words back at me.

"I was jealous. I didn't mean it, and I sure as hell don't care who or how many people you have fooled around with. Except Mason. I care that you kissed him, even if it was before we became a thing. I'm sorry for what I said."

She waggled her eyebrows. "I didn't kiss him. I was just curious to see if you felt the same way about him as he does about you. Because if you didn't realize it already, I'm pretty sure he's in love with you." Mel tossed me her keys. "What he said to you was not cool, but I think you two might be more alike than you realize. It can be easy to be owned by your emotions if you don't own them instead."

"How did you get to be so wise?"

"Just putting the psychology minor to good use."

"Knock, knock," I said, standing outside of Noah's room. "Your teammate let me in." It just happened to be Calvin, who had seemed more than eager to know what Mel had said about him.

"Hey, Jules." Noah lingered in his doorway, his expression shuttered.

"Can I come in for a minute? I owe you an explanation and an apology."

With a grimace, he stepped back to let me in. His busted lip looked painful. So did the bruise on his cheek.

"How are you feeling?" I paused just inside door until he waved me in. His room was neat. A plaid bedspread was pulled up over his bed.

"I've been better. Been worse."

"I'm really sorry."

"You weren't the one throwing punches." Noah sat on the edge of his bed.

"No, but you thought I was just like your ex, so you went to warn your friend."

"Only I didn't figure out until too late that he was the guy in the video."

"Worked that out on your own?" I laughed, but it fell flat.

"Mason's reaction was a giveaway once I had time to think about it. I can't say that I blame him. I should probably apologize. It makes me come off as a creep that I kept watching because she reminded me of you. That's not being a good friend."

"That is creepy." But who was I to judge because I had watched plenty of Mason's videos myself. "How about we don't bring up the videos ever again."

"If you're worried I'm going to say anything, I won't."

"Have you been to the med center?"

"I don't have practice until Saturday. This is a rest week. I'm hoping most of this heals. If I go to the medical center, it will go in my file, and if it's something that could get me benched, I might miss my chance with the scouts."

"I'm so sorry, Noah. Can I look at it?" I let my bag slide off my shoulder and pulled out the tub of salve I'd brought. "I brought the balm I use for sore muscles. It's good on bruises, too." I rub a little on his cheek. "Are your ribs sore?"

"A little." Noah leaned back as I pull up his shirt to up rub salve on a bruised spot across his ribs.

"What the fuck?" Mason's voice made us both tense.

"It's not what it looks like." Noah was the first to speak.

"I came here to apologize to Noah," I said, forcing the brittle words out. "He doesn't want to go to the med center and chance getting benched for the next game. I'm just putting balm on the bruises."

"He can't reach his own ribs?"

Stiffly, I stood and turned to face Mason. "I've had enough of whatever this is. The possessive routine—"

"He isn't exactly wrong," Noah chimed in. "I guess I owe you another apology, Jules."

"What?" I looked over my shoulder in time to catch Noah's sheepish expression.

"My ribs do hurt—"

"He knew I was coming," Mason said, his eyebrows lowering, "and just wanted to rub it in my face."

"I take back my apologies. You're both assholes." I capped the balm and set it on the bed.

Mason shook his head. "You're mad at me

when Noah knowingly set you up to make me jealous again?"

"You had it coming," Noah said. "I didn't realize it was you in the video. I was just trying to warn you." Noah winced pulling his shirt down.

"You know what? Have fun playing doctor on yourself." I grabbed the balm and chucked it at his chest.

"Don't act like you're the only one with the right to be mad," Mason called after me as I left the room.

"Mason, stop being so thick-headed," I growled walking faster down the hallway.

"Me? You are the most obtuse woman I have ever met!" Mason caught up to me.

"Excuse me?" I turned to find myself toe to toe with him.

"You are the most infuriating person I know. I swear to God, some days I wish you never moved in." His words cut me open. "You were never part of the plan, and yet here you are, ruining it."

"You are the jackass that kept saying it was nothing! You say I'm the obtuse one!" I snorted, pretending to hold onto my anger when my heart was shattering.

"I didn't think you'd stay if I said I wanted more!"

We were a hot mess. I swallowed, trying to decide what to say next. I knew what I wanted to say, but my brain refused to cooperate. Instead of replying, I stood there like an idiot as the silence stretched on, becoming thick.

"I'm just going to go." One of Noah's teammates slowly moved around us, making me realize the scene we were creating in the hallway. I continued down the hall and out of the building.

Mel was right. I was a coward. I hadn't realized how rigid my life was while I'd stayed inside my neatly drawn little lines, making plans. Mason was the first reckless, unplanned thing I had done in my life.

"I wasn't trying to interrupt and be a possessive asshole." Mason's voice brought me to a halt just as I started to open Mel's car door.

"It really wasn't what it looked like. I came by to apologize, but then I was going to find you. We need to talk."

Mason followed me back to Mel's, who was conveniently out. The car ride helped my temper but did little to settle my nerves.

"Mel told me she kissed you freshman year."

Mason's eyes widened. "She admitted it was a lie —*after* I said some really nasty things that made me understand that jealousy can make people say awful things. I'm not saying it's right, but I understand you didn't mean what you said yesterday."

Mason dragged a hand through his hair. "I regretted the words as soon as I said them. I regretted fighting with Noah, too. He thought he was helping me."

"Yet you looked like you were ready for round two today."

"You make me crazy." Mason closed the distance between us. "I've always liked you. Once you moved in, it became more. I know I was the one who suggested the videos, and I'll never regret sleeping with you, but it messed with my head. I never knew if you were happy with me, or if it was all for the money."

"What?"

"Everyone I've ever loved has left me, Jules. My parents. My grandma. I got used to being a loner because I didn't want to make friends and lose them. But I was always drawn to you. Even before you moved into Chelsea's, I'd noticed you on campus."

Did he mean…?

"You said you didn't want your future wife to know about the videos. We never talked about a future, so I assumed that meant we were short term, until you were finished making new content."

His gaze burned into mine. "I don't want anyone else."

"I don't want anyone else, either."

Mason pulled me to his chest, tilting my chin up so our mouths could meet.

"I love you, Juliet," he muttered the words against my lips. "I love cooking with you. I want more movie nights with your parents. I want to see you open your own kitchen."

Stunned into silence as a future I never considered before suddenly began forming. My heart soared looking at the man in front of me. The life we could build together. "I love you, too."

EPILOGUE

The sound of crying roused me from sleep. With a groan, I elbowed my husband in the side. "It's your turn," I mumbled, knowing I'd be getting up, too.

Mason mumbled something unintelligible as he climbed out of bed. We both swayed a bit as we made our way down the hall. By the time we turned on the nursery light, both babies were crying, demanding bottles and fresh diapers.

"I bet this wasn't exactly what you thought our honeymoon would be," I whispered as I rocked one of my baby brothers back to sleep. I smiled as I watched Mason burp my other sibling before settling back into the rocker next to me.

"You were right. Your parents deserve a mini

vacation, and this is good practice for us. Sometime in the distant future…." Mason yawned.

We eloped just after graduation. As a double surprise to my parents when we'd returned from Iceland as Mr. and Mrs., we'd offered to watch Jake and Jamie for Memorial Day weekend, so they could enjoy a trip of their own.

"Kids are in our future, but I'm not ready to share you with any more people anytime soon."

We'd put out a few more videos. Mason had hit his retirement goal. He still worked from home coding. I had finished my degree but started working with a catering company. One that specialized in meal preps for a local athletic team.

"I don't know how your parents manage with so little sleep." Mason yawned again.

"Did you not notice the amount of coffee in the pantry? It's right next to the formula." I chuckled, rising slowly to put Jake back in his crib.

"What do you think your parents are doing right now?" Mason had wanted to book them a vacation somewhere special. I think he'd been worried they'd be upset about miss our wedding.

"Are you kidding me? They're sleeping. I know I plan to do nothing but sleep when we get back home." It was my turn to yawn.

In the end, I had convinced him to swap houses for the weekend. The home office had been remodeled before we'd left for Iceland, fully converting it into an actual home office for Mason. My bedroom was back to being the guest room.

"True. Where do you want to go for our honeymoon?" Mason leaned over, kissing me after settling Jamie in his own crib.

"We eloped. I didn't think we got a honeymoon." I leaned into my husband as we both watched the sleeping babies.

"It's our life, we can make it whatever we want."

A NOTE FROM THE AUTHOR

Jules and Mason were a fun couple to write. It was enjoyable writing Jules falling in love. I have ideas for Mel in the future so there is a possibility we will see this couple again. My next releases are planned and will keep me busy for a while. This book started as a palate cleanser several years ago when I needed something light and fun while finishing my debut series. People always ask how ideas come to me for my stories and this one was just my quirky personality wanting to put a character is a bunch of scenarios that are both hilarious and embarrassing. This was pre pandemic and I wasn't sure if I was funny enough on the page to try a RomCom. I was nervous because it was a jump in genre but this book was fun to write and it helped remind me why I do this. I enjoy making characters and stories that readers can enjoy.

ACKNOWLEDGMENTS

Sometimes being an author is a very solitary gig. It can mean skipping events to meet deadlines and long hours in my hours. But it takes a team to create truly great stories.

I couldn't spend hours on my desk if it wasn't for my family being supportive. It's my husband bringing my tacos and handling the household chaos. My mom always ready to help and read no matter how weird she finds it to read sex scenes written by her daughter.

I like to think I have a thick skin but I couldn't keep publishing without my readers. I am grateful for all of you.

I cannot thank Sahara Kelley enough for creating such a great cover. Or my editor, Delilah Devlin, enough for her work helping me make this the best it can be.

I know I am forgetting people that page is far too short. For everyone I've missed I apologize, but thank you.

ABOUT THE AUTHOR

Cindy Tanner loves pizza, reading, and dreams of one day retiring to a mountain cabin with her family and getting a pet donkey. When she isn't on TikTok watching videos of fainting goats she is probably at her desk working on the latest project, chauffeuring her son, or getting distracted by one of her dogs.

ALSO BY CINDY TANNER

When You Were Mine

Mine For Now

Say You'll Be Mine

Made in the USA
Monee, IL
25 April 2022